Nancy Drew®
in
Mystery at the Ski Jump

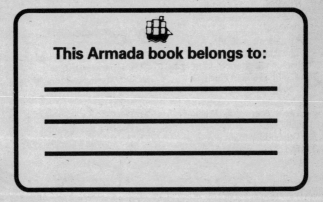

**This Armada book belongs to:**

## Nancy Drew Mystery Stories® in Armada

1 The Secret of Shadow Ranch
2 The Mystery of the 99 Steps
3 Mystery at the Ski Jump
4 The Spider Sapphire Mystery
5 The Clue in the Crossword Cipher
6 The Quest of the Missing Map
7 The Clue in the Old Stagecoach
8 The Clue of the Broken Locket
9 The Message in the Hollow Oak
10 The Invisible Intruder
11 The Ghost of Blackwood Hall
12 Password to Larkspur Lane
13 The Bungalow Mystery
14 The Whispering Statue
15 The Haunted Showboat
16 The Clue of the Dancing Puppet
17 The Clue of the Tapping Heels
18 The Clue in the Crumbling Wall
19 The Mystery of the Tolling Bell
20 The Clue of the Black Keys
21 The Clue of the Leaning Chimney
22 The Scarlet Slipper Mystery
23 The Secret of the Golden Pavilion
24 The Secret in the Old Attic
25 The Ringmaster's Secret
26 Nancy's Mysterious Letter
27 The Phantom of Pine Hill
28 The Mystery of the Fire Dragon
29 The Mystery of the Moss-Covered Mansion
30 The Hidden Staircase
31 The Mystery of the Ivory Charm
32 The Mystery of the Brass-Bound Trunk
33 The Clue of the Velvet Mask
34 The Clue in the Old Album
35 The Witch Tree Symbol
36 The Moonstone Castle Mystery
37 The Secret of Mirror Bay
38 The Double Jinx Mystery
39 Mystery of the Glowing Eye
40 The Secret of the Forgotten City
41 The Strange Message in the Parchment
42 Mystery of Crocodile Island
*
51 The Triple Hoax
52 The Flying Saucer Mystery
53 The Secret in the Old Lace
54 The Greek Symbol Mystery
55 The Swami's Ring
56 The Kachina Doll Mystery
57 The Twin Dilemma
58 The Captive Witness
59 The Mystery of the Winged Lion
60 Race Against Time
61 The Sinister Omen
62 The Elusive Heiress
63 The Clue in the Ancient Disguise
64 The Broken Anchor
65 The Silver Cobweb
66 The Haunted Carousel
67 Enemy Match
68 The Mysterious Image
69 The Emerald-Eyed Cat Mystery
70 The Eskimo's Secret
71 The Bluebeard Room
72 The Phantom of Venice

*For contractual reasons, Armada has been obliged to publish from No. 51 onwards before publishing Nos. 43–50. These missing numbers will be published as soon as possible.*

Nancy Drew Mystery Stories®

# Mystery at the Ski Jump

Carolyn Keene

Armada

First published in the U.K. in 1971 by
William Collins Sons & Co. Ltd, London and Glasgow
First published in Armada in 1976

This impression 1988

Armada is an imprint of
the Children's Division, part of
the Collins Publishing Group,
8 Grafton Street, London W1X 3LA

Printed and bound in Great Britain by
William Collins Sons & Co. Ltd, Glasgow

# CONTENTS

| CHAPTER | | PAGE |
|---|---|---|
| 1 | THE STRANGE WOMAN | 9 |
| 2 | A SERIOUS LOSS | 15 |
| 3 | MISSING EARRINGS | 22 |
| 4 | MORE TROUBLE | 29 |
| 5 | THE SECOND NANCY | 36 |
| 6 | CURIOUS DEALINGS | 47 |
| 7 | THE TV TIP-OFF | 56 |
| 8 | TRAPPER'S STORY | 62 |
| 9 | A DISASTROUS JUMP | 72 |
| 10 | A SURPRISE ANNOUNCEMENT | 82 |
| 11 | THE PASSWORD | 91 |
| 12 | SLIPPERY SIDNEY | 97 |
| 13 | THE HOUSE PARTY | 106 |
| 14 | THE FUR THIEF | 113 |
| 15 | RACING A STORM | 119 |
| 16 | AN S O S | 124 |
| 17 | THE HIDDEN CABIN | 129 |
| 18 | A WEIRD LIGHT | 134 |
| 19 | ZERO HOUR | 142 |
| 20 | THE TABLES TURNED | 148 |

# MYSTERY AT THE SKI JUMP

# ·1·

## The Strange Woman

"BRR-R, it's cold!"

Nancy Drew shivered and pulled the collar of her coat higher against the driving snow. Determinedly, she ducked her head and pushed along the darkening street, a new pair of skis slung over one shoulder.

Suddenly, out of nowhere, a long black car skidded across the pavement directly in front of the red-haired, eighteen-year-old girl.

"Oh!" Nancy cried out, leaping back just in time to escape being hit. A second later the car crashed into the porch of a nearby house.

As Nancy dashed forward to see if the driver were hurt, the door of the house flew open and the excited owner, Mrs Martin, rushed out.

"What happened?" she called. Then, seeing the car, Mrs Martin ran down the snowy steps. "Is someone hurt?"

Nancy had already opened the door on the driver's side. A slender woman in a fur coat was slumped across the steering wheel.

"Help me bring her into the house," Mrs Martin directed. Nancy laid down her skis. Together they carried the unconscious stranger inside and put her on a sofa in the living-room.

"I believe she's only stunned," Nancy announced, pressing her fingers to the victim's wrist. "Her pulse is regular and the colour's coming back to her cheeks."

"Just the same, I think we should call Dr Britt," Mrs Martin said nervously. "Will you do it, Nancy? The phone's in the hall. I'll get a blanket from upstairs to put over this woman."

Nancy went to call the doctor. The line was busy and it was a few minutes before she could get a connection.

"Dr Britt is out," the nurse reported, "but I'll give him your message."

"Thank you."

Mrs Martin came down the stairs with a blanket and Nancy told her Dr Britt would be there as soon as possible.

"Doctor! Who wants a doctor?" an annoyed voice called from the living-room. "I certainly don't need one. Say, how did I get here?"

Nancy and Mrs Martin were amazed to see the woman driver sitting up on the sofa. She was removing a make-up kit from the pocket of her coat. She calmly began to powder her face and dab on some exotic perfume as Mrs Martin explained what had happened.

"It was the storm," was all the unexpected visitor said.

Quickly Nancy appraised the woman. She was about thirty-five, strikingly handsome with blue-black hair, pale skin, and high cheekbones. An expensive-looking mink coat was draped nonchalantly over her slim shoulders.

"Why, Mrs Channing," Mrs Martin said suddenly. "I didn't recognize you. I'm glad you feel better. Nancy, this is Mrs Channing from the Forest Fur Company.

"Mrs Channing, I'd like you to meet Nancy Drew. She lives here in River Heights with her father, a famous lawyer. And Nancy herself is one of the best young detectives I ever—"

"Lawyer—detective!" Mrs Channing cried out. There was such a sharp expression in her dark blue eyes when she looked at Nancy that the girl felt slightly embarrassed.

"At least Dad is a fine lawyer," Nancy said, smiling. "Sometimes he asks me to help him on his cases. Your work must be interesting, too, Mrs Channing. I've never heard of the Forest Fur Company. Where is it?"

"Oh, we have many branches all over the country." Mrs Channing started to rise from the sofa but fell back weakly.

"I think you really should see a doctor," Nancy suggested kindly. "You're still shaky from the accident."

"I'll be all right!" Mrs Channing answered emphatically. "Perhaps if I could have a cup of tea—"

Nancy turned to Mrs Martin. "I think I'd better run along," she said.

"Oh, it's so cold outside, do stay and have some tea with us. It won't take a minute."

"Thank you, but I really can't," Nancy replied. "I'm leaving with Dad on a trip in the morning and have a lot of packing to do."

Nancy was looking forward to helping her father on a case in Montreal and enjoying some skiing. He had promised to tell her about his work at dinner that night.

A few minutes later she was shaking the snow from her coat and boots on the back porch of the Drew home. Opening the kitchen door, she called, "Hi, Hannah! I'm back."

"Well, I'm certainly relieved," replied a motherly voice from the hall. "What a storm! Did you buy the skis?"

"Yes, I did. They're real beauties. I can't wait to use them in Montreal."

Nancy recalled with pleasure her skiing weekend there the previous winter. What a wonderful feeling to stand on top of the mountain, in the cold crisp sunny morning, with the white world below her! Then off—down the fast trail to the bottom, concentrating on every turn and twist as the challenging trail demanded. Nancy had become so proficient that she had won the novice ladies' slalom race, successfully turning through all the slalom gates, in the fastest time.

Nancy smiled to herself as she thought of the "slalom gates", which were really just flags on tall poles stuck in the snow. Funny-looking "gates"!

The Drews' middle-aged housekeeper walked into the kitchen and smiled affectionately at Nancy. Hannah Gruen had been with the family ever since Mrs Drew had died when Nancy was a small child.

"I was delayed by an accident." Nancy explained what had happened. "I'm afraid Mrs Martin's porch will need a lot of repairing."

The conversation was interrupted by a telephone call from Nancy's friend, Ned Nickerson, inviting her to a fraternity dance at Emerson College the next month. She accepted gaily, then went upstairs to start packing. Five minutes later Hannah bustled into the bedroom.

"Look what I have to show you!" the housekeeper exclaimed.

Nancy's eyes gleamed. "A mink stole! It's beautiful!"

"It was such a bargain, I couldn't resist it," Hannah explained excitedly. "I've always wanted a fur stole but never felt I could afford it."

Nancy took the fur piece and laid it around her own shoulders. "It's gorgeous," she said. "Where did you buy it?"

"From a simply charming woman," Hannah replied. "She represents the Forest Fur Company. You see, she had already sold a stole to my friend Esther Mills. And Esther suggested—"

Nancy was not listening. At mention of the Forest Fur Company, her thoughts went racing back to the mysterious Mrs Channing.

"Nancy, do you think I was foolish?" the housekeeper asked anxiously as the girl frowned.

"I'm not sure," Nancy answered absently. "It does look like a good fur piece. But it's an odd way to sell expensive furs."

"I hope everything's all right," said Hannah, a worried look replacing her former eagerness. "I also invested some money in Forest Fur Company stock. The woman, a Mrs Channing, sold me ten shares. I paid her fifty dollars for it. But I'm sure it's okay. I have the certificate in my bureau drawer."

"Where is this woman staying?" Nancy asked.

"Why, I don't know. She didn't tell me."

At that moment Nancy heard the front door close and the sound of her father's footsteps in the hall. She put her arm about Hannah's shoulders and gave her a comforting squeeze.

"Don't worry. I'll run down and talk this over with Dad," she assured the housekeeper. "Perhaps he knows the Forest Fur Company."

"Hello, dear." Tall, handsome Carson Drew met his daughter at the bottom step and kissed her. "Do I detect a worried look in those pretty blue eyes?"

"Well, something's on my mind," Nancy admitted. She told her father about Mrs Channing and the Forest Fur Company.

"I've never heard of the firm," the lawyer remarked when she finished. "But I certainly don't like the way they do business. No reliable company would peddle expensive furs and stock from door to door at bargain prices. Please ask Hannah to let me see her certificate.

After reading it, he admitted it looked all right, but added that he thought the company should be investigated.

"Mrs Channing must still be at Mrs Martin's," Nancy said excitedly. "Suppose I go over there and talk to her."

"Fine." Carson Drew nodded. "I'll join you. We can't let our Hannah be taken in by swindlers."

The Martin home was only two blocks away. As the Drews reached it, Nancy noticed that Mrs Channing's car was gone. She dashed up the broken porch steps and rang the bell hurriedly. The door swung open.

"Mrs Martin," Nancy asked, "has Mrs Channing left already?"

"Yes." Mrs Martin's eyes blazed. "To put it bluntly, Nancy, Mrs Channing ran out on me. When I brought that tea she asked for, she was gone. And her car too! And not one word did she say about paying for the damage she did to my porch!"

"What's her address?" Nancy asked quickly.

Mrs Martin looked startled. "I don't know!"

# ·2·

## A Serious Loss

MRS MARTIN invited Nancy and her father into the house and offered them chairs before the crackling blaze in the fireplace.

"I suppose I'll never find Mrs R. I. Channing," she spluttered. "But that Forest Fur Company will pay for repairing my porch! Don't you think they should, Mr Drew?"

"That depends on whether or not Mrs Channing was using a car of theirs, or at least was doing business for them at the time of the accident. Suppose you tell us everything you know about this woman."

Before Mrs Martin could start, they heard the sound of heavy feet on the porch stamping off snow. This was followed by the sound of the door bell. The caller was Dr Britt, tired and cold after his long drive through the storm. When he learned that the accident victim had left in such a rude way, the physician was indignant.

"I don't blame you for being angry, Mrs Martin," he agreed, stepping into the living-room. "Anyone as ungrateful as Mrs Channing doesn't deserve sympathy. Good evening, Mr Drew. Hello, Nancy."

Mrs Martin indicated a fourth chair facing the fire. "You sit here and rest, Doctor," she urged. "I was just going to tell what I know about Mrs Channing.

"She came here two days ago and sold me a mink boa and some stock in a fur company. She promised that the stock would make me a great deal of money. But now I don't trust her. You know what I think? That she ran away from here because of you, Nancy."

"What!"

"Before I went to get the tea," Mrs Martin explained, "I told her how many cases you had solved yourself— not just for your father. Now that I think of it, I believe Mrs Channing got scared and left. We'll never find her."

"Mrs Channing also sold a mink stole and some stock to our housekeeper, Hannah Gruen," Nancy volunteered. "That's why I came back here."

Dr Britt looked thoughtful. *"Channing—Channing!"* he murmured. "I thought that name sounded familiar. Now I remember. My nurse, Ida Compton, showed me a fur piece and a certificate for stock she had purchased from a woman named Channing."

"This is very interesting," Mr Drew spoke up. "Nancy, why don't you see Miss Compton and find out if she can give you some additional information about Mrs Channing?"

"I certainly will, Dad. But by the time we get back from Montreal—"

"I suggest that you stay here a couple of days and see what you can find out," the lawyer said. "You can follow me later."

He rose, adding that Hannah Gruen probably was becoming uneasy over their absence. She would want to know what they had learned about Mrs Channing.

"And the delicious dinner I smelt will be spoiled," Nancy said, smiling.

"Let me drive you," the doctor offered. "Fortunately

the storm is dying down. It should be fair by morning."

When the Drews arrived home, Mrs Gruen met them with questioning eyes. They told her the truth but begged her not to worry about the fur company stock.

"It may be a good investment," the lawyer said cheerfully, although he doubted it. "And now, how about some food? This is the best eating place in the country, Hannah."

The housekeeper beamed. "Tonight it's pot roast and big browned potatoes exactly as you like them."

"Dessert?"

"Your favourite. Apple tart with lots of cinnamon." Mrs Gruen turned to Nancy. "Bess Marvin phoned. She's coming over after dinner. And George—I never can get used to a girl with a boy's name—will be here too."

"Great!" said Nancy. "The three of us will hold a farewell party for you, Dad."

Bess and her cousin George Fayne arrived at eight o'clock. Clad in boots and ski pants, they were in the highest spirits in spite of the cold. George, a trim-looking girl with short, black hair and an athletic swing to her shoulders, was the first through the door.

"Isn't this storm something? she exclaimed. "Old Man Winter is certainly doing his best to blow our town off the map." She panted. "One more big puff and I'd probably have landed on top of a church steeple."

Bess giggled. "That would be something—you flapping about like a weather vane!"

"Bet I could point in all directions at once," George retorted.

"Well, I'd rather stay inside," said Bess, blonde and pretty. "Maybe we can make some fudge," she added hopefully. Bess loved sweets and worried little about her weight.

"I'm afraid there won't be time for fudge," said Nancy. "The fact is, I have some work for both of you."

"Nancy! You don't mean you're on the trail of another mystery?" George asked eagerly.

"Could be," Nancy answered, her eyes twinkling. Quickly she briefed her friends about Mrs R. I. Channing and her questionable method of selling stock and furs.

"I've just been examining the stock certificate she gave Hannah," the young detective went on. "It gives the headquarters of the Forest Fur Company as Dunstan Lake, Vermont. But, girls, I've looked in the atlas and there's no such place as Dunstan Lake, Vermont."

"Too small, maybe," George suggested.

"Dad has a directory published by the Post Office Department," Nancy went on. "It's not in there, either."

"Then it must be a phoney outfit!" Bess declared.

"Perhaps," Nancy agreed. "Anyway, I must find that Mrs Channing as soon as possible."

"We'll help you search," George said eagerly. "Just give the orders!"

"Okay." Nancy grinned. "Suppose you two call all the garages in town and see if anyone brought in a long black car with damaged front fenders. Meanwhile, I'll use the private phone in Dad's study and call the local inns and motels to see if a Mrs Channing has registered."

When the girls met again twenty minutes later, all of them reported complete failure. Because of the weather, Bess and George were sure Mrs Channing could not have driven far. She probably had stayed with a friend.

"Unless she registered at a hotel under another name." Nancy mused.

Mr Drew joined them in a farewell snack, then kissed Nancy good night. He told her he would be gone before the three girls were awake, then asked:

"What's your next move?"

"To call on Ida Compton."

The next morning was crisp and sunny. Giant snow-ploughs, working all night, had effectively cleared the roads. At ten o'clock the three girls were seated in Nancy's sleek convertible, on their way to consult the nurse. Nancy pulled up at Dr Britt's office.

After hearing the story, Miss Compton was eager to co-operate. She explained that a few days previously, a tall, muscular man of about forty and his wife had called to see the doctor. They had given their names as Mr and Mrs R. I. Channing.

While they waited to see the doctor, the nurse had expressed her admiration for the mink stole Mrs Channing wore. To her surprise, the woman had removed the fur and offered to sell it cheap. She had also suggested Miss Compton buy a block of Forest Fur Company stock.

"Mrs Channing doesn't miss a trick, does she?" George remarked. "Always on the lookout for clients!"

"Mrs Channing seemed pleasant and honest." The nurse sighed. "Are you sure she isn't?"

"Well, I haven't proved anything yet," Nancy admitted. "But Mrs Channing's methods are very strange, and I couldn't locate Dunstan Lake."

Miss Compton said she never left the office when strangers were in it. But at Mr Channing's request she had gone to make a cup of tea because his wife felt faint.

"I'm afraid the tea business was just an excuse," Nancy said. "Those two wanted you out of here for some special reason. But why?"

The young detective's glance passed swiftly about the room and came to rest on a steel cabinet. "Of course!" she exclaimed. "The Channings wanted to look in the file. They hoped to get names and addresses of persons they might sell to."

"I guess that's true, Nancy," the nurse admitted. "Because as soon as Mrs Channing drank the tea and I handed her a cheque for the stole and the stock, she said they couldn't wait to see the doctor and hurried away."

"Miss Compton, will you do me a favour?" Nancy asked. "Call a few of the doctor's patients on the telephone right now. Ask if a Mrs Channing—or at least a dark-haired woman—has called on them, offering to sell them stock or furs."

She had no sooner made her request than the nurse began to dial a number. Within a few minutes Nancy learned that several patients had made purchases from a smooth-talking woman named Mrs Channing. Nancy spoke to each one but picked up no further information.

"I think we had better be on our way," she said finally. "I don't want to take any more of your time, Miss Compton. But if you will continue to check the people in those files, we can stop in later for the list. Somewhere there's bound to be a person who can give us a real clue."

"Where do we go from here?" George asked as the three friends got into the convertible.

"I don't know," said Nancy. "It's too near lunch-time to make any calls and—girls!"

Nancy's voice was excited as she bent over the steering wheel and stared down the street. "There! Just crossing the intersection in that car," she gasped. "I believe it's Mrs Channing!"

As soon as the light changed, Nancy turned left to follow the black car. She trailed it down the side street for a block, then on to a highway that led to open country. All at once the girls heard the warning wail of a siren. A police car drew up alongside the convertible. The driver waved Nancy to the kerb.

"Where do you think you're going in such a hurry?" the officer demanded.

"Oh!" Nancy flushed. "I'm sorry if I was going too fast. You see, I was trying to catch another car."

The policeman ignored her apology. "Let's see your driver's licence."

"Certainly, Officer."

Nancy reached for the wallet in her inner coat pocket. She snapped open a flap and suddenly her face was the picture of dismay.

Her driver's licence and all her other identification papers were gone!

## Missing Earrings

"Now, young lady, I suppose you're going to tell me you lost your driver's licence?"

The policeman's tone was sceptical as he looked at Nancy. The man was a stranger to her, which was unusual, since Nancy knew most of the local police and all were her friends.

"Oh dear! This is certainly a disaster!" wailed Bess. "Now we can't catch that awful Mrs Channing."

George spoke up. "Officer, this is Nancy Drew," she said. "We're after a thief. Please let us go."

The policeman stared. "You're what? Listen, miss, if that's the case, there are two reasons for my taking you to headquarters. Suppose you tell the chief your story." He directed Nancy to follow him.

Chief of Police McGinnis was surprised to see Nancy. He listened while she explained her predicament of being without a licence.

"I just can't figure out what happened to it," she continued. "I know I had it in my purse yesterday."

"I'm aware you have a driver's licence, Nancy," the chief assured her. "That's why I'm going to be lenient in your case. You've helped the police department on so many occasions that it's almost as if you were a member of the force."

At this remark the traffic policeman's jaw dropped.

"Oh, thank you, Chief McGinnis," Nancy said gratefully. "I'll make application for a duplicate licence at once."

"Good." The officer nodded. "But remember, young lady, keep your car in the garage until that new licence arrives."

"Chief, I have a driver's licence," Bess interrupted. "See—it's right here in my handbag. I can drive Nancy's car for her."

"You girls!" Chief McGinnis laughed. "You don't miss a trick, do you? Yes, Miss Marvin, I suppose you can act as chaffeur. And now what's this about a thief? Are you up to something we police don't know about?"

Nancy's eyes were teasing as she answered, "I'll let you know the instant I find out."

As the girls left, George exclaimed, "Whew, that was close! I thought you were going to have to tell him about Mrs Channing and I knew you didn't want to yet."

"No, not until I have some proof she's dishonest." There was a thoughtful frown on Nancy's brow. "I wish I could figure out what happened to my licence."

"You don't suppose someone stole it, do you?" Bess asked as she slid in behind the steering wheel.

"I can't decide," Nancy admitted. "In the first place, that licence isn't worth a thing to anybody but me. So why would it attract a thief? And why would he want my identification papers?"

"Maybe the thief was looking for money and took the other things by mistake," George suggested. "Did you have much money in your purse?"

"No, just an emergency five dollars," said Nancy. "I

have another purse that I carry silver and bills in. That wasn't tampered with."

"Well, we can put our heads together at lunch," said Bess. "You're both invited to my house. And, girls, I promise chicken pie and angel cake."

The food was delicious, but what interested Nancy even more was a message for her from Bess's father. Hearing of the case, Mr Marvin had telephoned his broker in New York and learned that no such organisation as the Forest Fur Company was listed among legitimate stock companies.

"Poor Hannah!" thought Nancy, deciding to redouble her efforts to find Mrs Channing.

That afternoon Nancy, Bess, and George stopped at Dr Britt's office and picked up the list Miss Compton had prepared. It contained the names of several patients who had bought furs or stock from the mysterious Mrs Channing.

"I think Mrs Clifton Packer would be a good one," decided Nancy. "She's a wealthy widow and bought several hundred shares of stock in the Forest Fur Company."

"Then, Mrs Packer, here we come," George said with a grin. "Step on it, chauffeur," she commanded, tapping her cousin Bess on the shoulder. "But for goodness sake—don't speed!"

The Packer house was a large stone building that looked more like a French château than an American residence. A maid, clad in a black uniform and a starched cap and apron, answered the doorbell. She ushered the three girls into the entrance hall.

Mrs Packer was a stout, talkative woman. She knew Nancy by reputation and was plainly curious as to the purpose of the young detective's call.

"Don't tell me I have a mystery here at Oak Manor, Nancy?" she began as soon as the three girls were seated in her luxurious living-room.

"Perhaps you have, Mrs Packer." Nancy smiled. She hastily sketched her reasons for suspecting Mrs Channing and her questionable sales activity.

"Why, I'm astounded—simply astounded!" gasped the plump widow. "Mrs Channing appeared so charming. Such a lady."

"I understand she sold you some furs," prompted Nancy.

"Oh, she did. She did indeed," babbled Mrs Packer. "And then, of course, there is that block of stock I bought. I paid her a thousand dollars for that."

Bess and George exchanged startled glances.

"Did Mrs Channing give you any information about this fur company?" Nancy asked. "Where it's located, for instance?"

"I don't think so," admitted Mrs Packer. "I just remember her saying they have mink ranches throughout the United States and Canada. That's why I thought the stock was all right. Good mink, you know, is very scarce. And very expensive."

"But suppose the stock you bought is worthless," said Nancy, and told what Mr Marvin had learned.

"Oh dear! I suppose I was foolish," Mrs Packer admitted. "But it was the lovely mink furs Mrs Channing showed me that convinced me. You see, I'm quite an authority on pelts.

"Come up to my bedroom, girls," the widow invited, leading the way. "I'll show you what I bought. All mink, you know, isn't equally fine. There are four different grades. The best fur comes from the northern

United States and Canada. It's the cold weather that makes it lustrous and thick."

Mrs Packer opened a wardrobe and removed a luxurious mink cape. "The minute Mrs Channing showed this to me I knew I had to have it," she rattled on. "Notice the rich dark-brown colour and how alive and silky the fur is!

"That shows the cape was made from young mink. In older animals, the fur is much coarser and the pelts are larger, too. A sure indication that you have a less valuable piece of merchandise."

George winked at Nancy. They were surely getting Mrs Channing's sales-talk secondhand!

Bess giggled. "Young mink, old mink—who cares?" she said. "I'd settle for any kind of a mink coat."

They went back to the living-room. Mrs Packer rang a bell and her maid, Hilda, a woman of thirty, appeared. She was asked to serve tea. After the maid had left, their hostess dimpled coyly.

"I just love tea parties, don't you?" Evidently she was not too concerned about her missing thousand dollars. "Hilda makes the most divine little cakes. I served them when I had the party for Mrs Channing."

"What!" George burst out, then added apologetically, "I'm sorry."

Mrs Packer explained that she had held a party for Mrs Channing to introduce certain friends who were always "looking for bargains in clothes". The friends had purchased both furs and stock. Nancy was about to ask their names when the woman abruptly changed the subject.

"Now that you're here, Nancy Drew, I want to consult you about the disappearance of my favourite earrings."

Nancy looked doubtful. "I don't know, Mrs Packer. I'm pretty busy just now. Perhaps you just misplaced the earrings."

"Of course I didn't," her hostess protested. "I always put everything back in my jewel case the minute I take it off. Besides, I was very careful of those earrings. They're part of a valuable set.

"See, I'm wearing the brooch that matches them. Nancy, how would it be if you take this with you, so you can trace the earrings for me?" the widow continued, removing the brooch and handing it to Nancy.

Despite the fact that the young detective had one mystery to solve and was to help her father on another, she found herself saying, just as Hilda walked in with the tea tray:

"I'll do what I can, Mrs Packer. When did you first miss your jewellery?"

As the woman pondered the question, Nancy saw Hilda stop short. The maid placed the tray on top of the piano and hastened back to the kitchen, as if she had forgotten something. Perhaps the napkins, Nancy thought, but she immediately noticed them protruding over the corner of the tray. Did Hilda's action have anything to do with the conversation?

"Do you remember when you missed your jewellery?" Nancy prompted Mrs Packer, who seemingly had not noticed the strange procedure.

"Oh, yes, now I remember," the woman said, her hands fluttering in agitation. "It was the day after that party."

George shot a glance towards Nancy, but let the young detective do the talking.

"Do you know of anybody at the party who might have wanted the earrings?" Nancy asked.

Hilda hastened back from the kitchen, picked up the tray, and approached her mistress. The maid was pale and nervous.

"No, unless it was—Why, Nancy, do you think it could have been Mrs Channing, the woman you said sold me the fake fur stock?"

At Mrs Packer's words an agonized wail burst from Hilda. She went chalk white.

"O-oh!" she cried.

Nancy looked up just in time to see the tray tilt precariously in the maid's hands. Hilda clutched at the dishes, but too late. The tray slipped from her grasp!

The lid of the teapot fell off and a cascade of hot water poured down upon the arm of Hilda's startled mistress. With it the cups and saucers clattered to the sofa.

Hilda, with a terrified scream, turned and ran from the room.

## ·4·

## More Trouble

"Oʜ! I'm burned!" Mrs Packer cried out. She jumped up and shook her wet sleeve. "Such stupid clumsiness!" she sputtered, seizing a napkin and swabbing her arm.

"Girls," she went on, "did you notice how Hilda jumped when I spoke of my stolen earrings? It's plain the girl knows something. Why, she may have taken them herself!"

"She certainly acted strangely," George agreed.

"Yes—and while we've been talking, she's escaped!" Bess added excitedly.

"Hilda looks like an honest person," said Nancy, coming to the girl's defence. "I think she's only worried or scared. Mrs Packer, do you mind if I look for your maid?"

"Go right ahead," the widow replied. "But I think I should call the police."

"Wait a little, please," Nancy urged. "And tell me, are there any other servants in the house?"

"No," said Mrs Packer. "My butler and cook have the afternoon off. If Hilda hasn't run away already, she's probably in her room. That's on the third floor. The second door to the left."

Nancy found Hilda's bedroom door tightly closed. But she knew by the sound of hysterical sobbing that the maid was inside. She knocked softly.

"Hilda, let me in," she called. "Don't be afraid. I just want to help you."

"Go 'way," said a muffled voice. "Mrs Packer—she'll fire me! She thinks I'm a thief!"

"No. I want to talk to you, Hilda," pleaded Nancy. "I'm your friend. Won't you listen to me, please?"

The sympathy in Nancy's voice must have convinced the nervous young woman, for she opened the door. "I was packing my suitcase," she admitted, dabbing at her reddened eyes with a handkerchief. "Oh, Miss Drew, I've been such a fool!"

"We're all foolish now and then," Nancy said soothingly. She led the maid gently to the bed and sat down beside her. "Hilda, why don't you tell me about it?" she suggested.

Ten minutes later Nancy and a subdued and calmer Hilda rejoined the others in the living-room. Nancy's blue eyes twinkled as she addressed her hostess.

"Mrs Packer, Hilda hasn't committed any crime. Her only mistake was that she did exactly as you did!"

"What do you mean?"

"Simply this," explained Nancy. "Hilda heard Mrs Channing tell you about the stock in the Forest Fur Company and how it would make you a lot of money. When she saw you buy some of it, Hilda decided to do the same thing."

"*Ja*," said Hilda, bobbing her white-blonde head. "That's just what I did. I think what's good for a smart lady like Mrs Packer is good for me."

Mrs Packer's grim face softened. "Why, Hilda," she said, "in a way, that's a compliment."

"Of course it is," said Nancy. "Hilda feels doubly bad because the money she used was the twenty-five dollars she borrowed on her salary to send to her family in Europe."

"Never mind," her mistress said gently. "I'll see that you don't lose by this, Hilda. Suppose you get busy now and clear away those broken cups and saucers."

Nancy and her friends left, the valuable brooch pinned on the young detective's blouse. She promised to try to find the earrings as soon as possible.

"I'm glad poor Hilda didn't lose her money and her job," said Bess as the three girls drove to Nancy's house. "I think Mrs Packer was to blame, anyway."

"We didn't get much farther in tracking down Mrs Channing," George remarked.

"No," said Nancy. "But I believe we've advanced a bit. We'd nearly forgotten Mr Channing. I'm sure that he's part of our puzzle."

"And what a puzzle!" Bess sighed as they drove into the Drew garage. She and George walked home.

Togo, Nancy's alert little terrier, was waiting for her when Nancy stepped into the house. The little fellow scampered joyfully ahead of her as she climbed the stairs and went into her father's deserted study. Togo cocked his head. He was hoping his mistress was going to play a game with him.

"I love this room, Togo," Nancy confided to him. "It makes me feel so close to Dad. Let's pretend he's here, shall we?" She sat down in the big leather chair and held out her arms to the eager dog.

"You sit right here—on my lap—Togo. That's it. Now we'll hold our conference.

"First of all, I know what Dad would advise. He'd say: 'Use your head, daughter! You can't just chase after this Mrs Channing as if she were a butterfly. You must outsmart her!'

"Hm-m, that's right," Nancy mused. "Probably Mrs Channing has exhausted her prospects in River Heights. This means she has moved into new territory. But where? Got any suggestions, Togo? Speak up, boy!"

At the word "speak" the little terrier gave a sharp bark. "Oh, I see." Nancy grinned. "You advise that we try one town in every direction from here. If Mrs Channing has been seen in any of these places, we'll know whether she has headed north, south, east, or west. And a very good idea it is."

Nancy heaved a sigh of relief and set Togo on the floor. "Okay. Conference is over," she announced. "Now we'll go and see about dinner, partner."

Nancy spent the evening at the telephone. First, she followed up the rest of the names on Miss Compton's list. No information of value came of this.

Next, she called several out-of-town physicians who were friends of Dr Britt. To her satisfaction, she found that three had been visited by Mr and Mrs Channing. Later the physicians called her back to say certain patients of theirs had been approached by the couple but only one woman had bought furs and stock. Three others, more cautious, had turned down the proposition. One of those, a saleswoman herself, had considered notifying the Better Business Bureau, but had not done so.

Before retiring, Nancy wrote a letter to the Motor Vehicle Department advising them of her lost licence. She hoped it would not be too long before a replacement was sent.

When Bess and George arrived the next morning, Nancy greeted them with, "We're going to Mason-ville. . . . Why? Because it's north of here."

"Nancy, it's too early in the day for riddles," George complained.

Nancy smiled mysteriously, then said all of Mrs Channing's victims to the west, south, and east of River Heights had been called upon at least a month before.

"So our saleswoman won't go back there," Nancy theorized. "But apparently she hasn't tackled Masonville yet. If we can only find her at work there—"

"Let's go!" George said impatiently.

Halfway to Masonville, Bess suddenly gasped. "Our fuel gauge says *empty*. I hope we don't get stuck."

Luck favoured the girls. A quarter of a mile further on, they came to a petrol station. The proprietor was a gaunt, grey-haired man in frayed overalls. Nancy lowered a window of the convertible and asked him to fill the tank. Then she said:

"Has a woman in a mink coat and driving a long black car stopped here lately?"

The old fellow looked at her shrewdly and scratched one ear. "Was the lady purty and was that a fine mink coat?" he countered.

At his words Nancy's heart gave an exultant leap. "Oh, you've seen her, then! Do you mind telling us when it was?"

"No, I don't mind," said the man. "The lady come by here yesterday mornin' on her way to Masonville. My wife was with me. The minute she spotted that coat she ohed and ahed, the way womenfolks do."

"Did she sell your wife a fur piece?" Bess interrupted, unable to restrain her excitement.

The man shook his head. "Nope. She didn't sell us nothin', young lady. But she claimed to be from a big fur outfit. Even offered to get my wife a mink coat cheap

—that is, if we'd buy some stock in her company first."

"Did she show you this stock?" persisted Nancy.

"She did, but I'm an old Vermonter myself. I never heard o' that town, Dunstan Lake, listed on the certificate."

"Did you ask her about it?"

"Sure, miss. She said Dunstan Lake was only a village with too few people for a post office. Sounded fishy to me."

"How right you are!" George said grimly. "I'm glad you didn't buy anything from her."

As the girls drove off, Bess exclaimed enthusiastically, "We're on the right track!"

Masonville was only five miles from the petrol station. The three young detectives were excited as they drove into town, convinced that they were on Mrs Channing's trail at last.

"Let's not celebrate too soon," Nancy cautioned. "Mrs Channing may have finished her work here and driven further north. But we'll investigate."

"I'll park in front of this bank," said Bess.

"All right," Nancy agreed. "We can walk from here. But first let's decide what to do."

"Shouldn't we try the hotels, Nancy?" George suggested. "If Mrs Channing is registered at one of them, it might save us the trouble of going to any other place."

"Do you know the names of the hotels here?" Bess asked.

Nancy thought a moment. "There's the Mansion House, but I don't think Mrs Channing would like that. It's a commercial hotel."

"Isn't the Palace in Masonville?" George recalled. "Famous for lobster or something?"

"Yes, but it's no longer a hotel, Dad told me. It's an office building now."

"We're getting nowhere fast," George groaned. "Let's go ask a police—"

She broke off abruptly as Bess's eyes suddenly grew wide with fear and she whispered excitedly:

"Girls! Look at those two men across the street! They're staring at us as if we'd just escaped from jail!"

"You're being silly," George remarked, not taking her scared cousin seriously.

"I mean it," Bess insisted. "You see for yourself."

George turned to look and Nancy leaned forward to observe the men. One was a short, stout man in a grey overcoat, with soft grey hair. The other was slim and younger. He wore a blue raincoat with the collar turned up, and a cap pulled low on his forehead.

At a nod from him, the stout man walked determinedly across the street towards the convertible, with the younger man close behind.

As the girls watched, the two men slowly circled the car and examined the licence plate at its rear. Then a big hand pulled open the door beside Bess.

"Which of you is Nancy Drew?" he demanded in a deep voice.

"I am," Nancy admitted. "Why do you want to know?

"You're wanted for shoplifting, Nancy Drew," said the stout man. "I place you under arrest!"

# ·5·

## The Second Nancy

THE man in the grey overcoat motioned the girls to get out of the car. For several seconds they sat still, too astonished to speak. Then Nancy faced the men and said calmly, "Suppose you tell me who you are and why you're making this ridiculous charge."

The stout man opened his coat. A police badge gleamed on his inside pocket. His companion showed one also.

"We're plain-clothes men," he explained. "We were told to pick up a car with this licence number and a Nancy Drew who owns it."

"You can't arrest Nancy!" Bess asserted.

George spoke up indignantly. "Nancy's a detective herself. You'd better be careful what you say."

The stout man looked grim. "Well, somebody detected *her* when she entered a fur store here and stole two expensive mink stoles."

"I did no such thing," Nancy declared quickly.

"Oh, yes, you did," the slim man insisted. "After you showed your licence and charged a cheap fur piece on credit, you took two expensive furs that you didn't charge! What did you do with them?"

Nancy realized that the woman who had her driver's

licence was pretending to be Nancy Drew! If it were Mrs Channing, she probably had altered the age and personal data on the card.

"Let's go to headquarters, girls," Nancy said. "We'll clear this up in no time."

At headquarters a sergeant took down Nancy's name and address. "Any relation to the lawyer in River Heights?" he asked.

"He's my father," said Nancy.

"Good grief!" Sergeant Wilks said, shaking his head. "You never know where these juvenile delinquents will come from!"

Nancy turned scarlet and George sputtered with anger. Neither noticed that Bess was no longer with them.

Suddenly the door was flung open. A distinguished-looking man hurried in, followed by Bess.

"Judge Hart!" Nancy cried, rushing forward to greet her father's old friend. "You're just the person I need!"

"That's what Bess tells me."

"You—you know the judge?" Sergeant Wilks stammered.

"Very well," said Nancy.

Judge Hart turned to the sergeant. "Why are you holding this young woman?"

The officer repeated the charges.

"There's a mistake somewhere," the judge insisted.

"It's because my driver's licence was stolen two days ago, Judge," said Nancy. "I've been telling these officers someone evidently is using it, but they won't believe me."

"I see." Judge Hart frowned. "Let's call in that

fur-shop owner and settle this matter properly."

The man was summoned to headquarters. He looked at Nancy and shook his head. "No, this is a different person. The thief was older."

"Was the woman wearing a mink coat, and did she have blue eyes and blue-black hair?" Nancy asked.

"Why, yes," the man said. "That describes her."

"Well, Sergeant," said Judge Hart, "is Miss Drew free to go now?"

"Certainly. Miss Drew, can you tell us where we might find the woman you spoke of?"

"I wish I could," said Nancy. "I only know that sometimes she calls herself Mrs Channing. Besides being a shoplifter, she sells fake stock."

"We'll be on the lookout for her," Wilks promised.

The girls walked with Judge Hart to his nearby office. Nancy thanked him for his help and told of the stock swindle.

"I've spent many summers in Vermont," the judge remarked, "but I've never heard of Dunstan Lake. Let me make a phone call and find out where it is."

The judge placed a call to the Vermont capital. When he finished his conversation, he declared, "There is no such place as Dunstan Lake anywhere in the State of Vermont. You have a real mystery on your hands, young lady. Let me know if I can help you."

"I surely will," Nancy promised.

As the girls walked back to the car, Bess asked, "Nancy, how do you suppose Mrs Channing got her hands on your licence?"

"Well, Mrs Martin and I left her alone on the sofa after the accident. When Mrs Channing regained consciousness and saw that we were out of the room, she must have slipped the papers out of my purse. It was in my coat on a chair."

"Shoplifters *are* quick with their hands," Bess pointed out. "Just like pickpockets."

Nancy nodded and said, "Well, girls, let's head further north!"

"North!" chorused the cousins in surprise.

"I'm sure Mrs Channing left Masonville right after that theft," Nancy answered. "She wouldn't dare turn back, so I believe she continued north."

The girls rode rapidly, stopping frequently at small towns to inquire if anyone had seen a woman of Mrs Channing's description.

At the town of Winchester, George went into the Crestview Hotel and soon came rushing back. "We've found her!" she cried. "The desk clerk says a dark-haired woman in a mink coat registered here last night. But she isn't in now."

"She's probably out robbing somebody," Bess remarked.

"And listen to this!" George said, growing more excited every moment. "Nancy, she's still using your name!"

Nancy's eyes flashed angrily. "I've always been proud of my name and I resent having it connected with a thief! Come on, girls. We'll wait for her in the lobby."

The three waited for an hour. Finally Nancy walked up to the desk. "We're here to see a guest registered as Nancy Drew," she told the clerk. "Do you suppose she came in another entrance?"

"That's impossible," the man said. "There's only the back door used by our employees. I'll ring her room if you like."

There was no answer to the call. Nancy decided to take the clerk into her confidence. When the man heard the story, he offered to unlock the suspect's room and see if there were any evidence that she was the thief.

"Please do that," Nancy asked the clerk, who said his name was Mark Evans.

When they reached the room, Bess and George remained in the hall to watch for Mrs Channing. Nancy followed Mr Evans inside. The man glanced about, threw open the wardrobe door, and cried out, "Her luggage is gone! She left without paying her bill!"

Nancy could detect the scent of the woman's exotic perfume in the air. The young detective walked to a window, lifted it, and stared at the ground below. The snow was marked with scrambled footprints and several deep indentations.

"I can see how Mrs Channing got away," Nancy said. "She slipped up here by the servants' stairway and dropped her bags out the window. Then she went down the stairs again, picked up her luggage, and hurried off."

"She can't be allowed to get away with this!" Mr Evans spluttered.

"Perhaps she left a clue that will help us find her," Nancy suggested. She moved slowly about the room, searching the floor and furniture. Methodically she opened and shut bureau drawers. All were empty.

Suddenly Nancy stooped to pick up something from beneath the bed. It was a small black label used by stores to identify their merchandise. The name on the label was : *Masonville Fur Company*.

"Here is a clue!" Nancy thought elatedly.

*"Here is a clue!"* Nancy thought elatedly

At the moment Nancy made her discovery a voice said, "What's wrong, Mr Evans?" The speaker was a plump woman who peered curiously into the room.

"Good morning, Mrs Plimpton," the clerk answered. "We're looking for a guest who occupied this room."

"Miss Drew, you mean," said Mrs Plimpton. "We ate breakfast together and had a nice chat."

Nancy suspected another stock sale. "I came a long way to see this woman," she said. "I wonder if I might talk with you privately."

"Why, certainly," Mrs Plimpton agreed. "My room's just across the hall. Come over there."

While George and Bess went to wait in the hotel lobby, Nancy listened to the woman's story. Mrs Plimpton had admired the fur coat which Mrs Channing wore. The younger woman offered to sell her a mink stole at half price.

Later that morning Mrs Channing had come to Mrs Plimpton's room and persuaded her to buy the fur stole. "But I didn't have the five hundred dollars she urged me to invest in her stock," the woman told her.

"Lucky for you," Nancy said, and explained that the value of the stock was questionable. "Mrs Plimpton, in your conversations with her, did this woman say where she might be going from here?"

The older woman shook her head. "I understood that she was to stay at Crestview for some time."

"Mrs Channing must have caught a glimpse of me as we entered the hotel," Nancy thought. Aloud she said, "May I see the stole?"

"Certainly," Mrs Plimpton replied, and brought out a fur piece. There was no label on it.

"Mrs Channing must have removed it," Nancy said

to herself. "But perhaps there's some other way to identify it as stolen goods." She explained her suspicions to Mrs Plimpton and asked to use the telephone.

Nancy called the Masonville Fur Company and learned that every fur piece sold there had MFC stamped on one of the skins. At the time of purchase, the date was added.

Nancy borrowed scissors and quickly opened the lining of the stole. Near the neckline was the MFC mark. There was no date.

"I'll let the fur company know," Mrs Plimpton said tearfully.

"I hope to recover your money," Nancy said. "By the way, that thief is not Nancy Drew. Her name is Mrs Channing. If you should ever see her again, be sure to call the police."

When Nancy joined her friends in the lobby, Bess suggested that they go to lunch at a tearoom she had noticed a few blocks away. As the three walked towards it, Nancy told what she had learned from Mrs Plimpton.

"Has Mrs Channing been doing this all along? Stealing furs and then selling them as a come-on for her fake stock?" George asked.

"I'm not sure where she got her first supply," said Nancy. "But evidently business has been so good that she ran out of merchandise and had to resort to shoplifting."

"Well, what next?" Bess asked.

"Before we leave town," Nancy said, "I'd like to canvass all the exclusive shops and find out if they've missed any furs or—" Her voice trailed away. She had seen an elegantly dressed woman with shiny blue-black hair walking briskly along the opposite side of the street.

"I'll be back!" she said quickly, hurrying across the street to follow the woman. Mrs Channing was moving so rapidly that the girl had no chance to trail her subtly.

Nancy had nearly caught up to Mrs Channing when the woman paused to look in a gift-shop window. An instant later she turned, ran down the street, and slipped into a small fur shop.

"She saw my reflection in that shop window!" Nancy thought, and walked rapidly to the fur shop. She gazed cautiously through the window. Mrs Channing was not in sight.

Nancy stepped inside. A small, stout man moved briskly to meet her, followed by a smaller and equally stout woman. "Something my wife and I can do for you miss?" the man asked.

"I came in to inquire about a woman I saw enter this place a minute ago," Nancy replied. "A tall woman in a mink coat. She has bluish-black hair."

The storekeeper raised his eyebrows and shook his head, at the same time glancing quickly at his wife. "Perhaps you are mistaken?"

"I saw her come in here," Nancy insisted. "I must find her."

"Who are you, please?" the man demanded.

"My name is Nancy Drew, and—"

With a yelp of rage the little man leaped towards the girl, pinning her hands behind her back. The woman threw a dark cloth over Nancy's head. Despite her resistance, the couple over-powered the young sleuth and dragged her to a back room.

"Unlock the cupboard!" the man directed.

Nancy heard the click of a door latch. She was shoved among some fur coats. The door slammed shut and a key turned in the lock.

"You'll never try to rob this store again!" the proprietor cried mockingly.

## ·6·

## Curious Dealings

THE cupboard in which Nancy was a prisoner was dark and stuffy. Fur garments crowded against her, nearly suffocating her. She pressed an ear to a crack in the door and listened to the murmur of excited voices in the shop.

"I say we call the police!" the woman shrilled. "Tell them we have captured this thief ourselves and no thanks to their protection!"

"But, Mama, suppose the lady in the fur coat was mistaken?" persisted the proprietor. "All we know is that she said a thief named Nancy Drew was coming to steal furs."

"And didn't Nancy Drew come in here?" insisted his wife. "That's good enough for me!"

Nancy heard the door of the shop open. "Pardon me," said a familiar voice. "Did a red-haired girl come in here?"

"George!" thought Nancy.

"Why do you ask?" the proprietor demanded.

"Because she's a friend of ours," Bess answered. "We saw her come into this shop."

After a moment of silence, the woman asked, "What's your friend's name?"

"Nancy Drew," George declared.

"You've come to help her rob us!" the woman shrieked. "Papa, lock them up too!"

Nancy doubled her fists and banged on the closed door with all her might. "Bess! George!" she shouted. "I'm locked in this cupboard!"

She heard a startled exclamation and the sound of running feet. In a moment the door swung open. "Nancy!" Bess gasped. "What happened?"

"Mrs Channing told these people I'm a thief!"

The proprietor frowned. "Mrs Channing?"

"The woman in the fur coat," Nancy told him. "She stole two mink pieces in Masonville yesterday. I believe she planned to rob you, but saw me coming and used this means to get rid of me."

"Nancy's a detective," Bess spoke up.

The mouths of the shop owners dropped open. "I meant no harm, miss," the man said quickly.

"Where did Mrs Channing go?" Nancy asked.

"Out the back door," The proprietor pointed. "I'm so very, very sorry—" he began.

"It's all right," Nancy said. "Come on, girls. Maybe we can pick up that woman's trail."

But Mrs Channing was not hiding in any of the alleys or shops in the vicinity. The three friends cruised up and down the streets of Winchester, and inquired at two other hotels and all the fur shops. No one had seen the woman.

Finally the girls decided to return home. When they stopped for petrol on the way back to River Heights, Nancy picked up a clue. She questioned the service-station attendant, who informed her that a long black car with dented fenders had stopped there for petrol a short time before.

"The driver was a dark-haired woman in a fur coat," the employee said. "I remember her because she seemed so nervous. Kept looking back over her shoulder all the time."

"Did she mention where she was going?" Nancy asked.

"No. But she said to fill her fuel tank—said she was starting on a trip. Maybe to Vermont, I thought. The car had a Vermont licence."

"Did you happen to notice anything she had in the car with her? Luggage or packages or anything?" George asked.

"Now, why are you girls so curious?" the man countered. "I'm pretty busy here."

Before Nancy could stop Bess, she revealed their suspicions of Mrs Channing. The attendant became cordial once more.

"You know, that woman did have two extra fur coats on the back seat," he said.

Nancy thanked the man for the information. While paying for the petrol, she asked, " Have you a telephone?"

"Yes, inside. Use it if you like."

Nancy phoned the local police, told what she had learned, and asked them to alert the Vermont authorities.

When Nancy finally reached home, Hannah greeted her with a broad smile and said, "I'm sorry you had such a long, tedious trip."

"Well, I picked up some good clues."

"What were you doing, anyway? Trailing that nice Mrs Channing?" Hannah asked.

"I wouldn't call her nice!" Nancy declared.

"Well, now, I think you're prejudiced," Hannah said. "That's fine stock she sold me!"

"What makes you think so?" Nancy asked.

"In the afternoon post I received some money from the Forest Fur Company—a nice, fat dividend," Hannah stated triumphantly.

Nancy stared at her in amazement. "That fake fur company actually paid you?" she asked.

"Yes, indeed!" said Hannah. "And Mrs Martin phoned to say that she received her payment, too."

"Why—why, it simply doesn't make sense," Nancy said, walking to the telephone. "I'm going to call Mrs Clifton Packer."

The wealthy widow greeted Nancy cordially, and admitted she had been mailed a sizeable dividend. But Mrs Packer did not sound pleased.

"I suppose the payment was not very large," Nancy remarked, thinking that the woman was no doubt accustomed to receiving sizeable dividends.

"It's not that," Mrs Packer replied. "Nancy, there's something queer about the way the money was sent. And one doesn't get dividends so soon after buying stock. I wish you'd investigate!"

Nancy's fingers tightened on the telephone receiver. "Something odd about the payment?"

"Yes," Mrs Packer went on. "As you might guess, I have stock in various companies. They all send their dividends by cheque. The cheques are signed by the treasurer of the company."

"And this payment was different?"

"It certainly was!" said the widow. "It was a money order posted from New York. No legitimate business would work that way."

Nancy thanked Mrs Packer for the information and hung up. "Well?" asked Hannah Gruen.

"Mrs Packer agrees that something is wrong," said Nancy. "Do you still have the letter that came with your dividend?"

"There wasn't any letter." The housekeeper frowned. "Just the money order in an envelope." Hannah said that she had cashed the money order and thrown the envelope away.

After a frantic search, Nancy located it in a wastebasket. She smoothed out the crumpled bit of paper to study the sender's name and address. There was no name, and the street number was blurred.

"Who sent the money orders?" she asked herself. "Not Mrs Channing—she was in River Heights at the time this was posted."

Nancy concluded that the woman must have a confederate in New York, someone to whom she sent lists of her victims and who then mailed the dividends. Could the person be Mrs Channing's husband? she wondered.

Nancy was eager to follow up the clue. "If Dad doesn't need me yet, I'll take the early plane for New York tomorrow," she decided.

After supper she telephoned her father and told him the news. "May I make a quick trip to New York before I join you?" she asked.

"If you think it's worth while, go ahead," the lawyer replied. "I've found some extra work up here that'll keep me busy a few days."

The next morning Nancy was optimistic as she boarded the aircraft. She always enjoyed trips to New York, which invariably meant a visit to Mr Drew's younger sister, a schoolteacher.

The slim, red-haired woman resembled Nancy in more than looks. Eloise Drew had assisted her niece in solving several mysteries.

Nancy took a taxi from the airport to Miss Drew's apartment. Her aunt greeted Nancy with a warm smile. "I was just hoping I could see you during my holiday next week!" she declared. "And here you are, and with that old twinkle in your eyes. You're involved in another mystery. Right?"

Nancy laughed. "Right! Will you help me?"

While she and her aunt prepared lunch, Nancy told of the case and the envelope clue.

"What do you plan to do next?" Aunt Eloise asked.

"Go to the address on the envelope. I think Mrs Channing's husband may be there. If he sent the money orders, I'll call the police."

"I'll go with you," Aunt Eloise announced.

After the two finished lunch, they started out. The address on the envelope proved to be that of a hotel in a run-down district.

At the desk in the lobby, a clerk glanced up as Nancy approached him. "Is a Mr R. I. Channing registered here?" she asked.

The clerk shook his head.

"Perhaps I was mistaken in the name," Nancy said quickly. "Have you a guest who works for the Forest Fur Company?"

The clerk grew impatient. "No, young lady. This is a residential hotel, and we don't handle business, so—"

"Did you mention the Forest Fur Company?" interrupted a voice behind Nancy.

The speaker was a red-haired woman in her early

forties. She was wearing a tight dress and too much make-up and jewellery. Nancy turned to her.

"I'm Miss Reynolds," the woman said. "I live here and I couldn't help overhearing you. I know the person you're looking for. I'm a stockholder in his company."

Nancy's heart leaped. She introduced herself and her aunt, and said, "Can you tell me where I can find the man you mentioned?"

"Why, he's Mr Sidney Boyd, and he lives in the suite next to mine!" the woman said loftily. "He is a true student of the theatre, Miss Drew. He said that my performance in *Wild Lilacs*—"

"I'm sure he was very complimentary, Miss Reynolds," Nancy interrupted. "But do you mind telling me how you happened to purchase stock in the Forest Fur Company?"

"Well, I had to coax Mr Boyd to sell it to me," the woman said coyly.

The clerk listened to the conversation. After Miss Reynolds nodded goodbye to the Drews and sauntered to the elevator, the man came over. "Hm!" he snorted. "Bunny Reynolds hasn't had a theatre engagement in years!"

"What about this Sidney Boyd?" Nancy prompted.

"Yes, tell us about him," Aunt Eloise put in.

"Ladies, I'm manager as well as clerk here. We don't want trouble on the premises."

"Then I imagine you want to avoid trouble with the law too," Eloise Drew said. "Suppose this Mr Boyd is involved in a stock swindle?"

"A swindle!" the manager gasped. "Well, I did suspect there was something phoney about that glib talker," he added defensively.

"What does he look like?" Nancy asked.

The man shrugged. "The usual ladies' man. Slender. Dark eyes. Kind of long, uncombed hair."

"He can't be Mr Channing," Nancy thought, "because he's a big broad-shouldered man." Aloud she said, "May I question some of your staff about Mr Boyd? It won't take long."

The man hesitated, then nodded. "Step into my office, ladies. I'll send the porters in first."

The men could tell nothing about Sidney Boyd except that he tipped generously. All the maids but one were unable to add anything. Katy, the fourth-floor maid, had such an uneasy manner of speaking that Nancy felt she might know something important about the suspect. She questioned the woman further.

"Mr Boyd gets up late," Katy said, growing more talkative. "Sometimes, while I'm waiting to clean up, he chats with me."

"What does he talk about?" Nancy asked.

"Oh, once he told me about when he was a little boy in Canada," said Katy. "He said his mother was French and his pa was a fur trapper—and he learned up there about furs. That's how I came to buy some of his fur stock."

"Forest Fur Company stock?" Nancy asked.

"Yes. I had a little money saved up," said Katy. "Maybe I shouldn't have spent it. But Mr Boyd wants to help me make more money. He says I'll get big dividends."

"Have you had any yet?" Nancy asked.

"No, but Mr Boyd promised some soon."

"The man's completely unscrupulous!" Eloise Drew cried out. "He swindles hard-working people like you!"

"Swindles?" Katy said. Tears began to stream down her face. "I've been robbed?"

"I think you'll get your money back," Nancy said soothingly. "Just try to tell me—"

Katy had already leaped to her feet. Sobbing, she flung open the door and rushed from the office.

Eloise Drew shook her head. "This is terrible. What do you propose to do next, Nancy?"

"See Sidney Boyd," the said grimly. "And turn him over to the police!"

As she and her aunt returned to the lobby, they heard the clang of the elevator door and the click of high heels.

"Wait! Please wait!" Bunny Reynolds called as she ran across the lobby towards the two. The woman's eyes were full of alarm. "Katy told me everything!" she wailed. "It's dreadful!"

"I'll try to help you—" Nancy began.

"And the earrings!" the actress interrupted. "What about the diamond earrings I bought from Sidney Boyd? I suppose they're worthless too!"

## ·7·

## The TV Tip-off

THERE was no quieting Bunny Reynolds. The woman was so agitated that Nancy and her aunt went with her to her room on the fourth floor.

Miss Reynolds paced the floor dramatically. "To think how I trusted that villain!" she lamented, flourishing her handkerchief. "Oh, oh, oh! I shall punish that unworthy soul!" The woman sank into a chair. "Only yesterday I let him sell me those no-good earrings."

"Are you sure the earrings are worthless?" Nancy asked.

"The stock's worthless. The earrings must be."

"Do you know where he got the earrings?" Nancy persisted.

"He said he inherited them from his mother and never intended to see another woman wear them until he met me. He said that only a woman of fire and artistic temperament should have them."

'I'm no jewel expert," said Nancy, "but I'd like to examine the earrings."

"Of course." Miss Reynolds went to her wardrobe. From a shelf she took a rolled stocking, which she unwound to disclose a small velvet-covered box.

Nancy took the case and opened it. *The case was empty!*

Bunny Reynolds let out a shriek. "He stole them!" she cried. "That horrible man took my money and then stole the diamond earrings!"

"It looks that way," Nancy said. "The diamonds must be real after all."

The actress burst into tears again. "I can't afford to lose all that money," she sobbed.

"Neither can a lot of other people who have bought Forest Fur Company stock," Nancy said grimly. "Miss Reynolds, what did the earrings look like?"

"Beautiful! Beautiful!" The actress sighed. "Tiny platinum arrows, tipped with diamonds."

Nancy opened her handbag and took out Mrs Packer's diamond brooch. "Were they anything like this?" she asked.

"Why," Bunny Reynolds exclaimed, "this matches the earrings exactly! How did you get it?"

"I'm afraid I have more bad news for you," Nancy said. "The earrings probably are part of a set that was stolen a few days ago from Mrs Clifton Packer in River Heights."

"Sidney Boyd robbed her, too?"

"I believe an accomplice of his—Mrs R. I. Channing—stole the earrings. Did Sidney Boyd ever mention her to you?"

"No," the actress answered. "Well, I'm going to call the police this minute!" She smiled coyly. "I have a special friend on the force," she said. "Police Sergeant Rolf."

Nancy spoke softly to her aunt. "I'm going to do some more investigating and see if I can find Mr Boyd," she confided. "Will you stay here with Miss Reynolds?"

Eloise Drew nodded. Nancy crossed the room. As she

flung open the door to the corridor, she collided with a crouching figure. Katy had been listening to the conversation.

Nancy smiled at the embarrassed girl. "Naturally you want to know what's going on, Katy."

"Yes, ma'am, I do," the maid said nervously. "Will the police get that awful man, Miss Drew—now that he's run away?"

"Run away!" Nancy exclaimed. "You mean Sidney Boyd has left the hotel?"

"His bed wasn't slept in last night," the maid said. "And all his things are gone. I didn't go in there till a few minutes ago because he had a *Do Not Disturb* sign on his door."

"Does the manager know this?" Nancy asked.

"I just told him," Katy said. "Mr Boyd checked out late last night. The night clerk forgot to report it to the day man."

"I'll bet he left right after he stole the earrings from Bunny Reynolds!" Nancy thought.

At Nancy's request Katy took her to the swindler's room. While the young detective investigated, a booming voice from the hallway announced the arrival of Sergeant Rolf. Nancy hurried to speak to him.

After hearing the actress's story, the tall sergeant asked to see the brooch which matched the stolen earrings. Nancy gave him the brooch and told him that Sidney Boyd had fled.

"The villain!" Miss Reynolds said bitterly.

The officer listened to the details of the case, then said, "I'd like to take the brooch to the police laboratory and have some photographs made. We can give the pictures to our men and alert them to be on the lookout in case Boyd tries to sell those earrings again."

"You're a remarkable detective!" Miss Reynolds cooed. "You'll get my money back, won't you, Sergeant? Right away?"

The man looked embarrassed. "Now, Miss Reynolds, it may take time," he protested.

The actress rolled her green eyes at him. "Can't you get some action by tonight?"

Sergeant Rolf fidgeted. "Well—er—the fact is that a lot of the men will be off duty tonight, Miss Reynolds. It's the Policeman's Ball."

The actress grew tearful. "You'll be dancing and having a good time while I—"

The sergeant took a deep breath. "Look, I've got no special lady friend," he said. "Suppose you come along with me?"

Bunny Reynolds was all smiles. "Why, Sergeant! How delightful! I'd love to go!"

Nancy beckoned to her aunt. "I think this is our cue for an exit." She chuckled. "If the sergeant will write a receipt for this brooch, we'll be on our way."

"Yes, ma'am." The officer wrote the receipt and gave it to Nancy. Then he made a note of her aunt's address and promised to return the brooch within a day or two.

"You certainly accomplished a lot, Nancy," Eloise Drew said when they entered her apartment. "And now, please relax for the rest of your visit. I've planned a special dinner tonight."

Later Miss Drew set the table with gleaming silver and tall lighted candles.

"I was so intrigued by your fur mystery that I ordered things for a trapper's dinner," she said.

When it was time to sit down to eat, Nancy was delighted. "How delicious everything looks!" she said. "Venison, wild rice, and my favourite currant jelly! Why, Aunt Eloise, this is a real north country feast!"

As they ate, their conversation returned to the mystery. "What was it you said about Dunstan Lake?" Aunt Eloise asked. "Is that the location of the Forest Fur Company?"

"So it says on the stock certificates," her niece answered. "But not even the United States Post Office has ever heard of such a place."

"Maybe it's not a town at all," Aunt Eloise suggested. "You know, Nancy, I recall that name from somewhere, but I can't remember when or how. I hope you'll let me help in your mysteries even though my memory's failed me!" she added with a chuckle.

"I call on you whenever I can," Nancy reminded her. "You've always been a help to me. Remember when you took my dog Togo to your summer home in the Adirondacks—"

"Togo!" Aunt Eloise interrupted. "I remember now. Someone came to the cottage while we were there. I believe he was a trapper. He was looking for a mink ranch and a Dunstan Lake. But there's no lake by that name around there. I remember thinking it might be the name of the owner of the mink ranch."

"That's a wonderful clue!" Nancy exclaimed.

"Please don't follow it tonight," her aunt teased, "or we'll be late for the theatre."

The next day Nancy and her aunt waited for word from the police. By evening they had received none, and Nancy finally declared that she could remain in New York only until noon the next day.

"Then I'll have to take a plane home in case Dad needs my help in Montreal. If the brooch hasn't arrived by that time, will you phone me as soon as it comes and then send it to me by registered mail?"

Aunt Eloise agreed, and the two spent the evening watching television. The late movie was an old film depicting a skating carnival. It began with a picture of the skating queen and individual close-ups of her ladies in waiting.

Suddenly Nancy cried out, "Aunt Eloise, look! That tall, dark-haired attendant!"

"She's very attractive," Miss Drew commented. "In fact, she's more striking than the queen."

"I know her!" Nancy cried.

"Friend of yours?"

"No, no. Aunt Eloise, she's the woman I'm trying to find. That's Mrs R. I. Channing!"

## .8.

## Trapper's Story

NANCY and Aunt Eloise waited eagerly for the motion picture to conclude. At the end the cast was named. Mrs Channing was listed as Mitzi Adele.

"Her stage name," her aunt guessed.

Nancy nodded. "Yes, or her maiden name. The film is seven or eight years old."

"She may have given up professional skating when she married," Eloise Drew suggested.

"Still, this helps," Nancy said. "If Mrs Channing was a skater, perhaps I can find some people in the profession who know where she comes from and something about her."

After breakfast the next morning Nancy phoned the television studio and asked for information about the skater Mitzi Adele. The man on the other end of the line advised Nancy to write to the Bramson Film Company, which had made the motion picture.

"Did you find out anything?" Aunt Eloise asked as Nancy put down the phone.

"Only the name of the film company. I hope they have that woman's address!"

Eloise Drew prepared to leave for school. Nancy thanked her for the visit and kissed her goodbye. After her aunt had gone, Nancy sent a telegram to the film company, asking that the reply be sent to her at River Heights.

As she was packing, the doorbell rang. Police Sergeant Rolf was in the lobby and asked to see her.

"I'm here to return that diamond brooch, Miss Drew," the officer told her. "If Sidney Boyd tries to sell the matching earrings, we'll get him!" The sergeant thanked Nancy for her help and left.

The weather was clear that afternoon and Nancy's flight was smooth. She took a taxi home from the River Heights Airport, and slipped quietly into the Drew home. Hannah was in the kitchen. Tiptoeing up behind the housekeeper, Nancy called loudly, "I'm home!"

"Oh!" gasped Hannah. "Nancy, you startled me!"

"Aunt Eloise sent her love," said Nancy as she removed her hat and coat and started for the hall cupboard. When she returned, Mrs Gruen was taking a pie from the oven.

"If Bess saw that cherry pie—" Nancy began.

"Bess and George have a surprise for you," Hannah interrupted. "Bess left word for you to phone her. George is there. Then tell me about the trip."

"I'll tell you first," Nancy said, laughing.

Ten minutes later she telephoned Bess, who reported that through a merchant who sold hunting equipment, she and George had met another investor in the Forest Fur Company.

"The old man's a fur trapper from up north," Bess went on. "He lives with his niece."

"When can I speak with him?" Nancy asked.

Bess consulted George, who took up the extension phone. "We'll drive him over tomorrow morning,"

George said. "That is, if we can persuade him to ride in a car. John Horn is strictly a high boot and snowshoe man."

Nancy laughed. "I'll get out my buckskin leggings and my coonskin cap!"

"We'll come early," George promised.

Mail for Nancy had accumulated on the hall table. As soon as she finished the conversation, she began to read it. Her duplicate driver's licence had arrived. There was also a note from her father, who was eager to have her join him.

"Did you see this?" Hannah asked, pointing to a telegram half-hidden by an advertising circular.

The message was from the Bramson Film Company. It stated that they did not know Mitzi Adele's address. However, a representative of the firm would call on Nancy shortly in regard to the woman skater.

"I wonder why," Nancy remarked. "Now I can't go to Montreal until I find out what the representative has to say!"

In the morning loud voices announced the arrival of Bess, George and the fur trapper. Stocky and round-faced the man strode up to the porch with the easy gait of a man of half his seventy years.

John Horn was dressed like Daniel Boone, Nancy thought, and his long white beard reminded her of Santa Claus. At her invitation, the three entered the Drew living-room.

The woodsman declined to take a chair. He stood before the mantel, his legs wide apart and his hands deep in the pockets of his heavy jacket.

"Well, young woman, what do you want to ask me?" he demanded, his bright blue eyes boring into Nancy's.

"Is it true that you bought Forest Fur Company stock from a Mrs Channing?" she asked.

"Yep. I was an old fool," John Horn admitted candidly. "I leaped to the bait—stupid as a wall-eyed pike!"

"I wonder if she told you anything that would help us trace her," Nancy said. "Did she mention a Dunstan Lake, for instance?"

The old man pulled at his beard. "No-o. Never heard that name, miss. All we chinned about was mink. I've worked on a mink farm and I been trappin' the little rascals for years. That's how I came by Arabella, here."

From a pocket in his coat, he pulled out a small, squirrel-like creature with bright black eyes and a long tail.

"Why, it's a mink!" cried Bess.

"Sure, she is!" John Horn said proudly. "Four months old and with as prime a pelt as I ever seen. Notice that glossy dark-brown fur? See how thick and live-looking the hair is? Arabella's an aristocrat. Yes, sir-ree!"

"Is she tame?" George asked.

"She's tame because I raised her myself," explained John Horn. "A wild mink, though, will bite—and his teeth are plenty sharp."

"Where did you get her?" Nancy asked.

"Arabella was born on a mink ranch. The first time I saw her she was a pinky white and not much bigger than a lima bean. All baby minks are like that. Tiny and covered with silky hair."

John Horn gave his pet an affectionate stroke and replaced her in his pocket. "You want me to help you catch that crook, don't you, Miss Drew?" he said.

Nancy had no such thing in mind  However, if the fur company was located in the Adirondacks, as Aunt Eloise believed, it would be handy to have an experienced woodsman around

"Mr Horn, I may need your help if I have to travel up north or into the mountains, she said.

"You can count on me!" said the old man.

"Excuse me, Nancy," said Hannah from the doorway. "I thought perhaps these folks would like some hot chocolate and cinnamon toast."

At the sight of the older woman, John Horn became ill at ease. "No, thank you, ma'am," he said hastily. "Fact is, I gotta be goin'."

"We'll drive you," Bess offered.

"No. No, I'd rather walk." The old trapper turned to Nancy. "I like you, girl. You—you talk sense," he stammered. "Here—take this!"

Nancy felt something warm and furry wriggle in her hands. Startled, she gasped and stepped backward, dropping the little mink to the floor.

Arabella instantly leaped away, straight towards the astounded Hannah. The housekeeper clutched at her skirts and hopped on to the nearest chair. "A rat!" she shrieked.

"It's a mink," Nancy said. She reached down and tried to catch the little animal.

"It'll bite!" Hannah warned. "Like a rat!"

Arabella was terrified by the strange surroundings and the squeals of Bess and Hannah. The tiny animal scuttled frantically here and there in search of a hiding place.

John Horn held up one hand. "Quiet, everybody!

You women stay put! And cut out that yammering! You'll skeer my poor pet to death!"

The trapper located Arabella crouched in a corner of the entrance hall. He spoke to his pet softly as he approached. Then, kneeling, took the mink into his arms.

Just then the doorbell rang. Nancy opened the door to a well-dressed, middle-aged man.

"How do you do?" he said. "Is this a bad hour to call? I've rung several times."

"I'm sorry," Nancy said. "We were chasing an escaped mink and we—"

"A mink?" The stranger stared at Nancy.

She blushed and pointed to the little animal nestled against John Horn's chest. "It's a tame mink," she said.

"I see," said the newcomer, still bewildered. "I'm Mr Nelson from the Bramson Film Company, and I'd like to speak with Miss Nancy Drew."

"I'm Nancy Drew. Please come in and sit down in the living-room. I'll be with you in a few minutes."

The man walked inside and Nancy turned to the trapper. "I'd love to keep Arabella," she said, "but I think she'd be happier with you. Besides, we have a dog here. That might make trouble."

Horn nodded, tucking the mink back into his pocket. "My offer to help catch that crook is still good."

Nancy smiled. "I'll call on you."

The cousins departed with Arabella and her master, who rode away in the back seat of Bess's car. Evidently he had changed his mind about walking!

Nancy entered the living-room and sat down.

"Miss Drew," said Mr Nelson, "I understand that

you want to find Mitzi Adele. Just how close a friend of hers are you?"

"Friend?" Nancy shook her head. "Not a friend."

After she had told what she knew of the woman, Mr Nelson's voice became more cordial. "I'm glad you told me this, Miss Drew," he said. "Frankly, we thought you might have been mixed up in Mitzi's dealings. A few years ago Mitzi stole several valuable costumes from the Bramson Film Company. We've been looking for her ever since."

"Do you know where she came from?" Nancy asked.

"Her home was in northern New York State. Somewhere near the Canadian border. That's all I know about her." After a little more conversation, the caller left.

Nancy went to the kitchen to tell Hannah what she had learned. "Now I must go to Montreal," she said. "In fact, I'll leave this evening if I can get a train reservation."

Nancy secured a sleeper on the late express and sent a telegram telling her father the hour she expected to arrive. Hannah helped her pack, and went with her in a taxi to the railway station.

Next morning Nancy looked out the window eagerly as the train pulled into the Montreal station. She hurried down the steps into her father's arms.

"Nancy! I'm so glad to see you!" he cried, taking her skis.

"I'm twice as glad to see you," she replied.

"How goes the great fur mystery?" Mr Drew asked as they followed a porter to the taxi stand.

"I'm stymied, Dad," Nancy admitted.

"Well, sometimes a change of work helps. Suppose

you give me a hand. A young man, Chuck Wilson, is my client here. I'm puzzled about him and I'd like your opinion. If you can, get Chuck to tell you about his case himself."

Nancy smiled. "When do I go to work?"

"You'll meet Chuck in an hour. I told him we'd be at the ski jump of the Hotel Canadien, where I'm staying."

"I'll have to go to the hotel first and put on ski clothes," Nancy said.

The hotel, a few miles out of the city, nestled at the foot of a majestic hill. Nancy was shown to her room, where she dressed in a trim blue ski outfit. Then she and her father went out to a nearby ski slope and ski jump. As they approached the foot of the jump, a man prepared to descend it.

The skier waited for his signal. An instant later he came skimming downward, fast as a bullet, only to rise into the air, soaring like a bird, with arms outstretched. He made a perfect landing.

"Good boy!" cried Mr Drew.

"That was beautiful!" Nancy exclaimed. "I wish I could jump the way he does."

"That's my client—perhaps he'll give you some instruction," said Mr Drew. "Chuck—Chuck Wilson— come over here!"

The slender youth waved. He stomped across to them, his blonde hair gleaming in the sunlight.

After Nancy's father had completed introductions, Chuck asked, "Do you ski, Nancy?"

"Yes. But not very well."

"Perhaps I can give you some pointers," Chuck suggested eagerly. "Would you like to come and ski with me?"

"A good idea," Mr Drew agreed. "I'll leave my daughter with you and get back to work. Take good care of her!"

"I sure will!" the young man answered in a tone that made Nancy blush. They waved goodbye to Mr Drew. Then Chuck Wilson seized Nancy's hand and pulled her towards the base of the jump. "I must see this next jump, he said.

The skier made a graceful take-off. Then something went wrong. The man's legs spread-eagled on landing and one ski caught in the icy snow, throwing him for a nasty spill.

The watching crowd gasped, then was silent. A spectator, a short distance away from Nancy and Chuck, rushed towards the man. "You idiot!" he yelled. "What will happen to Mitzi if you kill yourself?"

Hearing the name Mitzi, Nancy elbowed her way quickly through the crowd. She was too late. By the time she reached the spot, the unfortunate jumper and his friend had disappeared.

"Why did you run off?" Chuck asked as he reached Nancy's side.

Nancy apologized. "I'm looking for someone. Can we go to the ski lodge? Perhaps he's there."

"Okay," Chuck said, leading the way.

The lodge was crowded with skiers but the men were not inside. Nancy asked Chuck if he knew the skier's name.

"No. But say, would his initials help?"

"Oh yes! Where did you see them?"

"On his skis—if they were his. Big letters."

Nancy's heart skipped a beat. "What were they?"

"R.I.C."

Nancy's spine tingled as if someone had put snow down her back. Could this be Mitzi Channing's husband? And the other man—was he, perhaps, Sidney Boyd?

# ·9·

## A Disastrous Jump

CHUCK WILSON chatted cheerfully as he and Nancy went up in the chair lift to the station where they were to begin their ski lesson. But Nancy's thoughts were far away. She kept wondering about R. I. Channing and whether her hunch was correct. Was Mitzi Channing's husband really in Montreal? Was he the mystery jumper?

"Maybe I should have tried harder to find him," she chided herself.

The ski instructor noticed her faraway look. When they reached their destination, he said:

"Time for class? Suppose you take off from here. I want to watch you do parallel turns down the practice slope."

Nancy gave a quick shove with her sticks and glided away.

"Not bad. Not bad at all!" Chuck called as she completed her trial run. "You have self-confidence and a fine sense of balance. Have you ever done any wedeln?"

"Yes," Nancy admitted. "But not very well."

"We can try some steeper slopes tomorrow," her companion said, smiling. "You shouldn't have any trouble. Now take another run. Remember always to lean away from the hill. Keep your skis together all the time. You need more of what the French call—abandon."

"Abandon?"

"You know—relax." Chuck smiled. "Bend your knees, keep your weight forward. You have a natural rhythm. Use it when you wedeln. It is just half turning in rhythm all the way down the hill."

When the lesson was over, Nancy turned to her instructor. "Thanks for everything," she said. "To-morrow I'd like to try some jumping. But now I mustn't take up any more of your time."

"My time is yours," Chuck said. "I have no more lessons scheduled for today."

Nancy was pleased. Perhaps she could get Chuck to forget skiing and talk about himself.

"I'd like to take you out to dinner tonight," he said, "and perhaps go dancing."

Nancy hesitated. The young man read her mind. "If your father would care to come—"

"Suppose I ask him," Nancy replied. She liked Chuck Wilson.

"Then it's settled," Chuck said. "I'll drive you back to the hotel now and be on hand again at six-thirty. Or is that too early?"

"Six-thirty will be fine," Nancy agreed.

Mr Drew was pleased when Nancy told him that Chuck Wilson had invited them to dinner, but he said that he would not go along.

"I'd rather have you encourage him to talk without me there," he said. "Sometimes a young man will talk more freely to a girl than to his lawyer. I feel Chuck has been holding something back. See if you can find out what it is."

Promptly at six-thirty Chuck walked into the hotel lobby and greeted the Drews. He expressed regret that Mr Drew was not joining them.

"Your daughter could become a very fine skier, Mr Drew," Chuck observed. "All she needs is practice."

"I've no doubt of it." The lawyer smiled proudly. "But I guess Nancy will always be better on ice skates than she is on skis. She was fortunate in having a very fine teacher. I sometimes thought he might encourage her to become a professional!"

"Why, Dad, you're just prejudiced," Nancy protested.

"If you like skating," Chuck spoke up, "how about going to see an exhibition that's being held here tomorrow night? I'm going to skate. If you could use two tickets—?"

Mr. Drew shook his head. "I'm afraid Nancy and I won't be here, my boy. Thank you, though. And now, I must leave you two."

Nancy wondered if her father's decision to depart from Montreal had anything to do with Chuck. Mr Drew had said nothing about their time of departure. In any case, she had better get started on her work!

It was not long before Nancy and Chuck were seated in an attractive restaurant. "Chuck," she said, "have you skated professionally very long?"

"Several years."

"Did you ever hear of a Mitzi Adele?"

"No, I never did. Is she a skater?"

Before Nancy could reply, the orchestra started a catchy dance number. Chuck grinned, rose, and escorted her on to the floor.

Nancy had never danced with a better partner. She

*"Chuck thinks he's skating,"* Nancy said to herself

was thoroughly enjoying it when suddenly Chuck seemed to forget he was on a dance floor. The musicians had switched to a waltz and Chuck became a skater.

He gave Nancy a lead for a tremendous step backward, then lifted her from the floor as if to execute a skating lift.

"Chuck thinks he's skating," Nancy said to herself.

But with a laugh he gracefully put her down again, continuing to dance. "What next?" she wondered.

Chuck swung round beside her and they glided arm in arm in skating style around the dance floor. He gave her a twirl, then the music ended. Chuck clapped loudly.

"Nancy, you're wonderful," he said.

Back at the table, she remarked that he must have been dancing all his life. Chuck looked at her searchingly for a moment, then said:

"My parents were dancers. Would you like to hear about them?"

"Oh yes."

"They were quite famous, but they were killed in a train crash when I was twelve years old. It stunned me and for a long time I wished I had died too. I had to go to live with an ill-tempered uncle. He hated dancing, and would never let me even listen to music."

"How dreadful!" Nancy murmured.

"That wasn't the worst of it," Chuck went on. He explained that only recently he had found out that his grandfather had left him an inheritance, but apparently it had been stolen from him by his uncle.

"Uncle Chad had a small ranch in the north country," Chuck went on. "He gave me a miserable time in my boyhood. My only friend was a kindly old

trapper. He took me on long trips into the woods and
taught me forest lore. It was from him that I learned to
ski and snowshoe and to hunt and fish, too. I guess
Uncle Chad became suspicious that the old man knew
about the money my grandfather had left me and might
cause trouble. So he scared him away.

"Later on, as soon as I was old enough, I ran off to
Montreal," Chuck continued. "And now I've asked
your father to be my lawyer. I want him to bring suit
to recover my inheritance."

"Dad can help you if anybody can," Nancy said
confidently.

"Yes, I know that. But it's such a hopeless case. I
have no legal proof of my uncle's dishonesty, Nancy. My
one witness has disappeared."

"You mean the old trapper?" Nancy asked.

"Yes." Chuck nodded. "And there never was a finer
man than John Horn."

John Horn! The name of the old trapper! Could
there be another such man besides the one in River
Heights?

Nancy decided to say nothing to Chuck of the possibility that she knew the one person who could help him.
After all, there was no need to arouse false hopes until
she had made a definite check.

Four hours later, after an exciting evening of conversation and dancing, Chuck left Nancy at her hotel,
with a promise to meet her at the ski lift the following
morning. She hurried to her father's room to tell him
her discoveries. The lawyer was not in, so Nancy
decided to make a long-distance call to her home in
River Heights. Hannah Gruen answered the telephone
but there was little chance for conversation.

"I can't hear a thing you say, Nancy," the house-keeper protested. "There are two jaybirds chattering at my elbow. I'm so distracted I can hardly think."

"Oh, you mean Bess and George?" Nancy laughed. "Put them on the line please."

"Nancy, I'm so happy it's you!" cried Bess an instant later. "George and I came over here to spend the night because we thought Hannah might be lonely."

"Besides, we had a feeling you might call," George put in on the extension phone.

"Tell us what you've been doing. Tell us everything!" Bess urged eagerly.

"Well, I had a skiing lesson this afternoon. My instructor was a client of Dad's named Chuck Wilson."

"And what did you do this evening?" Bess persisted.

"Chuck and I had dinner together, and danced, and talked."

"And I suppose this Chuck Wilson is young and very good-looking?" Bess asked. Nancy could detect disapproval in her tone.

"He is." Nancy chuckled. "But I don't see—"

"I'm thinking of Ned Nickerson," Bess reproached her. "Don't you break Ned's heart, Nancy Drew!"

"Nonsense," Nancy countered. "Now listen carefully, Bess. I have a job for you and George. I want you to see that old trapper, John Horn. Ask him if he ever knew a boy named Chuck Wilson."

"We'll do it first thing tomorrow," Bess promised.

Nancy was up early the next morning. At breakfast she told her father Chuck's complete story, ending with the item about the old trapper.

"That's a stroke of luck for us." The lawyer nodded.

"If your man proves to be our missing witness, Chuck Wilson may really have a case. You've done a fine job, my dear. Are you seeing Chuck today?"

"I'm meeting him at the ski lift at ten."

"Well, have a good time. I'll join you at lunch. By the way, we have reservations on the five o'clock train."

"I'll be ready."

Chuck Wilson was waiting for Nancy at the ski lift. "You're going to enjoy jumping," he predicted. "It's a great thrill and it might come in handy someday if you're schussing a mountain and you suddenly come upon a sizeable hummock.

"Now there's a slope with a big mogul in the middle. Moguls," he explained, "are big lumps of snow formed by many skiers turning in a certain path on a steep slope. The more the steep area is used for turning, the bigger the lumps or moguls become. Suppose we climb up there and have a go at it."

"Just tell me what to do," Nancy urged.

"The first thing to remember is that when you hit a bump it will lift you into the air," Chuck cautioned. "Your job is to crouch down before you hit your obstacle. You spring upward and sort of synchronize your spring with the natural lift the bump gives you. Is that clear, Nancy?"

"I think so."

"Good! Then here are a few other rules," Chuck continued as they reached the crest of the little hill. "Try to pull your knees up under your chest as you jump, Nancy. And push down hard on your heels so that the points of your skis won't dig into the ground and trip you. Hold the upper part of your body erect and balance with your arms outstretched."

"That's a lot to remember," Nancy replied. "I'd feel better if there weren't so many people milling about the hill. When I come down, I want a clear track."

"Oh, you'll be okay," Chuck assured her. "All you need is practice. Well, Nancy, this is it. Don't use your sticks. I'll hold them. Get set— GO!"

In an instant Nancy was off. Flying gracefully as a bird down the long, smooth slope, she watched the snow-covered bump ahead of her loom larger— LARGER. And then, suddenly, her heart skipped a beat, and she gave a gasp of dismay.

"A snow bunny!" Nancy exclaimed.

The inexperienced skier ahead floundered directly into her path, stumbled, and fell just over the edge of the mogul. Nancy had to choose between jumping over his prostrate body or crashing into him.

*She must jump!*

Nancy crouched and sprang upward, jumping as far as she possibly could. She came down in a heap.

Chuck Wilson cried out as she spilled, and sped down the slope to his pupil's rescue.

"Nancy! Nancy!"

The girl lay motionless!

# ·10·

## A Surprise Announcement

"Nancy! Are you hurt?"

She opened her eyes slowly and looked up into Chuck Wilson's worried face. He was kneeling beside her and chafing her wrists.

"W-what happened?" she asked in a faint voice.

"You spilled," Chuck explained. "You made a clean jump over that skier and then you pitched on your face. But it wasn't your fault."

"Not my fault? You mean that man—"

"He got in your way, all right," Chuck answered. "But it was a loose binding on one of your skis that caused your fall." The instructor showed it to her.

Nancy sat up. "I want to try again," she said.

"Do you think you should?" Chuck asked.

"Of course I should!" Chuck helped Nancy rise to her feet. "See?" She smiled. "No bones broken. Nothing injured except my dignity!"

For the next hour, Chuck helped Nancy with her jumps. "You're learning fast!" he declared. "I wish you didn't have to return to the States so soon. Can't you persuade your father to stay, at least until after the ice show tonight?"

"Maybe I can," Nancy said. "I have an idea!"

"Please try!" Chuck beamed. "Here are some tickets

to the ice show. I'll expect to see you and your father there tonight."

"I can't promise," Nancy reminded him. "But thanks! So long for now, Chuck. I'd better go back to the hotel and meet Dad."

Nancy and her father had a late lunch in the hotel dining-room. The lawyer looked amused when his daughter told him she wanted to stay longer in Montreal. "For the winter sports or for young Wilson?" he teased.

Nancy made a face, then grew earnest. "I'm thinking mainly of the Channings," she said. "They may be selling more of that fake stock right in this area!" She told about the expert ski jumper and her suspicion that he was R. I. Channing.

"Mrs Channing may be here too," the lawyer mused. "Yes, I think we ought to stay until you can investigate. Will you still have time for that skating exhibition tonight?"

"Of course!" Nancy said. "That's part of my plan. Have you forgotten that Mrs Channing is a professional skater—or used to be one?"

Mr Drew smiled. "You think this woman may attend the show, or even take part in it?"

"Exactly. And if she does show up. I think I have enough evidence to have her arrested. Even if she's not there, I may be able to get some information about her from the skaters."

The head waiter suddenly appeared. "Pardon me, but are you Miss Nancy Drew?" he inquired. When she nodded, the waiter said, "There's a long-distance call for you in the lobby."

Nancy excused herself and hurried to the telephone.

The caller was George Fayne, who told her excitedly, "Bess and I just spoke with John Horn. He remembers Chuck Wilson!"

"George, that's marvellous!"

"And he says that if he can do anything to help Chuck, he's willing to go to Canada!"

"That's just what I'd hoped for!" said Nancy. "I'll be home soon and tell you all the news."

"Another mystery?" George asked.

Nancy laughed. "This one is Dad's. I'm just helping!"

She returned to the table and told her father of John Horn's offer.

"Now, that's progress!" the lawyer declared. "I'll tell Chuck as soon as possible. Meanwhile, Nancy, why don't you do some sightseeing in Montreal this afternoon?"

"A fine idea!" Nancy agreed. "I can combine sightseeing with a visit to fur shops and hotels."

Nancy walked around the picturesque city all afternoon, but did not find a clue to the Channings at the fur shops she visited. By the time she returned to the hotel it was early evening, and heavy snow had begun to fall.

"It's a good thing the ice show wasn't planned for outdoors," Mr Drew remarked as he and Nancy waited for a taxi.

When they were seated in the big arena, Nancy studied her programme and saw that Chuck would skate first. Neither Mitzi Adele nor Mitzi Channing was listed. "Perhaps she's among the spectators," Nancy thought. She borrowed binoculars from the man seated next to her and carefully scrutinized the audience.

Nancy concluded that Mrs Channing was not present. "I'm afraid my guess was wrong, Dad," she sighed.

"Mrs Channing might be using another name, or be wearing a disguise," Mr Drew suggested.

"If she does appear," Nancy mused, "I'd like to know how to reach the police in a hurry."

"Just go to one of those little black boxes along the wall," her father said. "They connect with a police booth in the balcony."

"Dad, how did you figure that out?" Nancy asked admiringly.

"I didn't," the lawyer said with a chuckle. "I called the police station this afternoon and asked what kind of protection they'd have here."

Suddenly the loudspeaker blared, "*Attention!* We have a late entry in the Pair Skating. Miss Nancy Drew and her partner from the United States."

Nancy's father turned to her in astonishment. "Why didn't you tell me you were going to skate?"

"Because I'm not," Nancy declared. "Mrs Channing must be using my name again!"

Nancy left her seat, her face flushed with anger. She followed signs that pointed the way to the skaters' dressing rooms. But as she neared the area, a uniformed attendant blocked her path. "Sorry, ma'am, nobody's permitted back there except skaters."

"But I'm Nancy Drew!" she protested, showing the man her driver's licence.

The attendant glanced at it, then stepped aside as he declared, "I thought Miss Drew came in before. Well, you dressing room is straight ahead. Your name is on the door."

Nancy found the corridor crowded with skaters in

colourful costumes. Mrs Channing was not among them.
Suddenly an eager voice exclaimed, "Nancy! Are you
looking for me?"

Nancy turned to see Chuck, who wore a black and
red pirate's suit. "No, Chuck. It would take some time
to explain why I'm here."

"So you entered the exhibition!" Chuck said. "I
wish you'd told me!"

"It's a mistake," Nancy said, moving on hurriedly.
"I'll explain later, Chuck."

She edged past the dressing rooms until she came to
one with her name on it. She knocked on the door.
There was no response. Nancy took a deep breath and
opened the door.

*The dressing room was empty!*

Nancy was crestfallen. She had missed Mrs Channing
again! A quick survey of the room convinced her that
the woman had been there recently. The scent of her
heavy perfume was thick in the air.

Had Mrs Channing been frightened away? Who had
warned her? Had she seen Nancy come into the
arena?

Nancy left the dressing room and made her way back
through the crowded corridor. She questioned the
skaters she met, but none recalled having seen the
woman she described.

Chuck Wilson greeted her again. "I have a solo part
in the first number," he told her. "I'd like you to see it.
You'll still have time to get into your costume."

"Chuck, I'm not going to skate—really!" Nancy said.
"I'm not the girl who signed up for the Pair Skating!"

"What?"

"Tell me, did you speak about me to anyone here

after that announcement on the loudspeaker?"

Chuck grinned. "Maybe I did mention to some of the performers that I know you," he admitted. "I said you were with your father in the arena."

"When you said that, were you standing anywhere near the dressing room with my name on it?"

"Well, I guess I was," Chuck replied. "Now, won't you tell me what all the mystery is about?"

"Not yet—not in this crowd," she said. "Too much has been overheard already!"

"*Is Miss Drew here?—Miss Nancy Drew?*"

A short, plump man with a waxed moustache came down the corridor, looking about him as he asked the question.

"That's Mr Dubois, the manager of the show," Chuck told Nancy.

"I can give you information about Nancy Drew," the young detective told the man.

Mr Dubois motioned to Nancy and Chuck to follow him to an unoccupied dressing room. "Tell me where this young woman is," he urged. "She must perform in thirty minutes."

"I'm sure she has left," Nancy said. "The woman who entered the exhibition isn't Nancy Drew at all. That's my name. This other woman is Mitzi Channing, and she's wanted by the police."

The manager threw up his hands. "The police! Are you saying that I've been sponsoring a criminal?"

"I know you've done nothing wrong," Nancy said quickly. "But surely you want to help catch a thief. Please tell me what you know about this skater. What does she look like?"

The description Mr Dubois gave identified the

woman as Mitzi Channing. She and a man named
Smith had come that afternoon to try out for the show.
Mr Dubois described the man, but Nancy did not
recognize him.

"They were excellent skaters," the manager said,
"and I gave them permission to enter the Pair Skating.
The woman wouldn't allow her partner's name to be
announced."

Nancy thanked Mr Dubois. Just then a bell sounded.
The manager and Chuck hurried off, and Nancy went
to a telephone to tell the police of her suspicions.

In the auditorium, Mr Drew was becoming increas-
ingly anxious about Nancy. Once he considered going
to search for her. "No." he told himself, "she works fast
when she has a lead, and I trust her to act intelligently."

The lawyer assumed that the late entry in the Pair
Skating would be scratched. He was surprised when
the announcer declared that the next skater would be
Miss Nancy Drew and that her partner would be
Charles Wilson.

Mr Drew watched his client, wearing close-fitting
black slacks and an open-necked white satin shirt, glide
gracefully on to the ice. Then the young man was
joined by a red-haired girl in a white satin ballet
costume.

The lawyer gasped. "*Nancy!*"

The two skaters danced in unison, then spun off to
skate individually. While Nancy executed some simple
steps, her partner jumped and whirled in intricate
patterns.

Nancy had conceived the plan while Chuck was
skating his first number. When he had returned to the
dressing room, Nancy had asked him, "Do you think I

danced well enough with you last night to try it on skates?"

"Why, sure! You're cool."

"I can't tell you the whole story now," Nancy had said, "but I'd like to take the place of that woman who called herself Nancy Drew."

The young sleuth thought, "Some of Mrs Channing's friends might be in the arena, unaware that the woman has left. When I come on instead, one of them may be so startled that he'll reveal himself. I'll ask the police to hold anyone who tries to leave the building during or immediately after the number."

Turning to Chuck, she had said, "Will you skate with me if Mr Dubois will let me and if I can borrow a costume and skates?"

"You bet I will!"

"I'm no expert," Nancy warned. "So don't try anything tricky. I'll leave the fancy steps to you, and while you're in the spotlight, I'll have a chance to do some detective work."

"To do what? Well, all right!"

Mr Dubois had agreed to the plan and a girl Nancy's size had offered to lend the young sleuth skates and a costume.

Nancy's heart had pounded with fright when the loudspeaker had announced their number. But with Chuck's confident voice encouraging her, she soon lost her nervousness.

At the end of the number, the young man grasped Nancy's wrists, swept her from her feet and spun round and round with her until the music blared the last note. Nancy was dizzy as applause rang in her ears.

As her vision cleared, she noticed that a tall, heavy-set man had risen from his seat and was moving quickly towards an exit. Was he R. I. Channing?

Nancy turned to her partner. "Come on, Chuck," she urged. "Let's get off the ice quickly. I think the mystery is about to be solved!"

# ·11·

## The Password

"WELL, here he is, Miss Drew!"

A big policeman thrust his prisoner through the open door of Nancy's dressing room.

"We've been watching for this fellow ever since you warned us that he might try to make a getaway," the officer went on. "He denies everything."

"Of course I deny it," the prisoner snarled, twisting away from his captor's grasp and glaring at Nancy. "My name is Jacques Fremont. I'm a respectable citizen of Canada, and I've never heard of R. I. Channing!"

The man was bluffing, Nancy felt sure. The tall, muscular body, the touch of grey at his temples—both tallied with the description of Mitzi's husband that Dr Britt's nurse had given.

"I suppose you have never heard of Mitzi Adele, either?" Nancy asked.

For an instant the man looked startled. Then his eyes met Nancy's in a glare of hate. "No, I've never heard of her either," he sneered. "See here, Officer, this is outrageous. I have an identification. Here's my driver's licence. It'll show that I'm Jacques Fremont."

The policeman looked at the licence in the man's wallet, then nodded. "Everything seems to be in order," he admitted. "I'm afraid that if you have no more proof than this, Miss Drew, we'll have to let the man go."

Nancy was taken aback. She was sure of her accusation. But there was nothing she could do but thank the officer for his trouble and watch as the man who called himself Jacques Fremont slammed angrily out the door.

"If only I weren't in costume and could follow him!" Nancy sighed, then looked up in relief to see her father standing on the threshold.

"Congratulations, daughter!" Mr Drew called. "I was never so surprised as when—"

Nancy did not let him finish. "Dad! Quick! That tall man you just passed—the one in the brown overcoat. Follow him!" she implored.

"But, Nancy—"

"I'm sure he's R. I. Channing. I asked the police to stop him," Nancy went on rapidly, "but Channing insisted his name is Jacques Fremont and they let him go. Oh, Dad, trail him, please!"

"All right, Nancy," the lawyer agreed, dashing off.

Nancy had just put on her street clothes when Chuck Wilson knocked on her door. "I thought perhaps you'd like to go out somewhere for a late supper, Nancy," he suggested. "After all that exercise, I'm hungry as a bear."

"I'd like to," Nancy replied. "But I must go to the hotel and see Dad as soon as he gets back. I'll tell you what. Suppose you drive me there and we'll have a bite in the coffee bar."

Once they were in the car, Chuck Wilson glanced curiously at Nancy. "I suppose I shouldn't ask why you were expecting the police?" he began. "You've shown me there are a number of things you don't care to divulge."

"I can tell you now," Nancy replied. "I'm trying to catch a woman who stole my driver's licence and goes around using my name. This evening I tried to have the police arrest her husband. But the man was too clever and they had to release him. Dad went to trail him, though."

"And you can't wait to get the report." Chuck grinned. "I don't blame you. To be honest, I was afraid your secrecy might have had something to do with my case. When the policeman went to your dressing room—"

"Oh, I'm sorry, Chuck. Didn't Dad get in touch with you this afternoon?"

"No. I wasn't at home. Can you tell me what he wanted?"

"I suppose I can. It's good news. Your old friend John Horn has been found," Nancy announced.

"What! Oh boy! That's great!" Chuck shouted, and yanked the steering wheel hard. In his excitement he had let the car head for a snow drift, and barely got out of the way.

When they reached the hotel, Nancy left word at the desk for Mr Drew to meet her and Chuck in the coffee bar. Half an hour later he came in and dropped wearily into a chair beside them.

"Mr Drew," Chuck spoke up, "Nancy says you've located John Horn."

The lawyer smiled. "Nancy did," he answered. "Actually, my daughter has done more on your case than I have," he confessed. "But as soon as we get back to River Heights, I'll see this man Horn and have a talk with him about your uncle."

"And what did you learn on my case, Dad?" Nancy asked. "Did you find Mr Channing?"

"I did and I didn't, if that makes any sense," her father replied. "Chuck, will you order me a hamburger and coffee while I start the story? That rascal Channing moves fast, Nancy. I spotted him soon after I left you, and almost caught up with him."

Nancy's face fell. "But you missed him?"

"Yes," her father admitted. "The man hopped into a taxi. But I did manage to get the car's licence number and later located the driver. He told me that Channing —or Fremont as he calls himself—went to the New Lasser Hotel."

"Oh, Dad, that's wonderful!" Nancy cried triumphantly. "All we need do is watch the hotel and wait for all the thieves to show up there."

"It isn't that simple," her father replied. "I talked to the manager of the New Lasser. He's a fraternity brother of mine and very friendly. He said that a Jacques Fremont, a Miss Nancy Drew, and Miss Drew's brother occupied a suite of several rooms on the second floor. Unfortunately for us, Miss Drew's brother checked out for the trio an hour before I arrived."

"Oh dear!" Nancy groaned. "Now we must start hunting for them all over again. Did you get any clues about where they went, Dad?"

Mr Drew took a bite of his hamburger sandwich, chewed it slowly, and swallowed before answering. Nancy knew from the twinkle in his eyes, though, that he had something important to reveal. Finally he spoke.

"It seems that Mitzi was expecting an important long-distance call at ten tomorrow morning. When she found she must leave town in such a hurry, Mitzi wrote out a message and entrusted it to the clerk. The message read:

" *'Foxes after stock. Transferring to camp.'* "

"What does that mean?" Chuck asked, puzzled.

The lawyer and his daughter shrugged, but Mr Drew prophesied that Nancy would soon learn the answer. Then he changed the subject.

"The performance you two put on this evening was most commendable," he said. "Nancy, I knew you were good on skates, but I didn't know you were that good."

Nancy smiled at Chuck. "I didn't know it, either!" she said.

The gay little party broke up soon afterwards. Mr Drew confessed to being very sleepy, but Nancy remained wide awake for hours. She kept thinking of the message Mitzi Channing had left with the hotel clerk, wondering about its true meaning.

At breakfast she joined her father in the coffee bar with a brisk air that indicated she had come to a decision. With laughter in her eyes, she said:

"Good morning, Dad, you old fox!"

"Fox?" Mr Drew raised his eyebrows in surprise.

"I was thinking of Mitzi," his daughter explained. "I believe when she wrote that message *'Foxes after stock,'* she meant us, Dad. You and I are the wily foxes."

"That might be," the lawyer admitted.

Nancy confided a daring plan she had conceived before going to sleep.

"Well, good luck," he said when she finished. "But be careful!"

Shortly before ten o'clock Nancy entered the lobby of the New Lasser Hotel, and strolled over to the telephone switchboard operator.

"My name is Drew. Miss Nancy Drew," she explained, displaying her duplicate driver's licence. "I'm expecting a long-distance call at ten o'clock—"

"But I was told Miss Drew had checked out," protested the operator. "In fact, the clerk gave me a message to deliver when the call comes in."

"I know," said Nancy. "I intended to leave town but decided to stay. I'll just sit here and you can let me know when the call comes through. That is, if it's not too much trouble."

"No trouble at all," said the operator. "Wait, Miss Drew. I think your party's on the line now. Take the end booth, please."

Nancy's heart was pounding as she hurried towards the telephone. So much depended on whether the person on the other end of the line was convinced that she was Mitzi Channing. Cautiously she lifted the receiver and said:

"Hello!"

"Hello," snapped back a man's brisk voice. And then it added a second word—"Lake."

For an instant there was silence. Nancy thought frantically. "Lake?" That must be a password between the swindlers, she told herself. Suddenly a possible answer snapped into her mind. She set her jaw and tried to make her voice sound coarse.

"Dunstan," she replied.

## ·12·

## *Slippery Sidney*

THE word "Dunstan" seemed to satisfy the man at the other end of the wire. He identified himself as Sidney.

"Listen, Mitzi!" he said. "I've got a deal cooking here for a thousand dollars' worth of stock. Old Mrs Bellhouse will buy it, but I've got to work fast."

"Swell," Nancy murmured in a low voice.

"Sure, it's swell," Sidney agreed. "But the trouble is, I'm nearly out of certificates. You'll have to get more printed and rush 'em to me!"

"You mean to River Heights?"

"Speak a little louder!" Sidney ordered.

"I said, where do you want the stock sent?"

"Why, to the Winchester Post Office, of course. General Delivery," the man snapped. "As soon as I make this sale, I'll beat it to Dunstan."

The receiver clicked as the man abruptly ended the conversation. Nancy hurried back to the Hotel Canadien, where she found her father waiting in the lobby.

"I'm glad you're here," he said. "I've been called home on urgent business. I've already notified Chuck that we'll be leaving on the next plane."

Nancy had no chance to tell about the man on the telephone until she and her father were seated in the plane.

"I'm sure I was talking to Sidney Boyd," she declared. "The one who sold stock and earrings to that actress in New York. And then stole the earrings from her!"

"Obviously you're right," the lawyer agreed. "But in order to trap this man, you'll have to supply him with new stock certificates."

"I know. Dad, would it be possible to make copies from Hannah's certificate?"

Mr Drew looked thoughtful. "I know a printer who would do a rush job for us. However, I must warn you that it's illegal to print fake stock even for a worthy purpose. I'll contact the authorities and get permission."

As soon as the plane landed at River Heights, Mr Drew went to his office. Meanwhile, Nancy searched several telephone directories for a listing of Mrs Bellhouse. There was none, so she went to the public library and thumbed through the city directories. Apparently no one by the name of Sidney Boyd's intended victim lived in Winchester or in any of the nearby towns.

At dinner Mr Drew reported that he had received permission to have Hannah's stock certificate copied. The printer would have the papers ready by noon the next day, and Mr Drew would rush them to Montreal where a colleague would remail them to Winchester.

"That's great," Nancy said. "But something worries me, Dad. I can't find Mrs Bellhouse's address anywhere."

"Never mind!" the lawyer reassured her. "As soon as those stocks are mailed, we'll notify the Winchester police. They can watch the General Delivery window at the post office and shadow Sidney Boyd after he picks up the package."

Nancy shook her head. "Mr Boyd may call for the package under another name. Perhaps Mitzi always sends the stocks that way."

"Well, ours will be addressed to Sidney Boyd, since that's the only name we know. Of course, the fellow may send someone else to the post office to get the parcel, and he may collect the money from Mrs Bellhouse before he goes to the post office. We'll have to remember that we're taking a gamble."

Nancy nodded. "But the odds would be with us if we could find Mrs Bellhouse and catch that man in the act of selling her his fake stock."

Hannah Gruen spoke up. "If this Mrs Bellhouse is elderly, she probably sees a doctor from time to time. Why not ask Dr Britt about medical people in the area who might know her?"

"A wonderful idea!" Nancy exclaimed, hurrying to the telephone. At her request, Dr Britt agreed to do this.

The next morning Bess and George arrived at the Drew home, eager to trade news with Nancy. George reported that John Horn had gone ice fishing, but would speak with the Drews as soon as he returned.

"He says Chuck Wilson's a right handsome fellow," she added.

Bess sighed. "Nancy has all the luck!"

"Well, wish that my luck holds out," Nancy said, smiling, "at least until Dr Britt contacts me." At that moment the telephone rang.

The caller was Miss Compton, Dr Britt's office nurse. She told Nancy, "Dr Green recently placed a woman named Mrs Bellhouse in the Restview Nursing Home, at the edge of Winchester. Visiting hours are between two and three-thirty."

Nancy thanked the woman and hung up. After telling the cousins what she had learned, she said, "Let's have a talk with Mrs Bellhouse."

The girls started off immediately. Just before two o'clock they reached the rambling white nursing home. A uniformed nurse greeted them and Nancy explained their mission.

"Can you come back tomorrow?" the woman asked. "Mrs Bellhouse has been ill and she's sleeping now. She shouldn't have callers today."

As the girls returned to the car, Nancy proposed that they stay near the nursing home to see if Sidney Boyd showed up. They waited an hour but the suspect did not appear.

The next day Nancy learned from the detective on duty at the Winchester Post Office that Sidney Boyd had not been there. "It's probably too soon," she thought.

At two o'clock Nancy and her friends were again at the nursing home. The nurse they had spoken to the previous afternoon led the girls to a sunny front room on the second floor.

Mrs Bellhouse was a fragile old lady with silver hair and faded blue eyes. She smiled as Nancy approached her bed. "Who are you?" she asked.

"I'm Nancy Drew, Mrs Bellhouse, and these are my friends, George Fayne and Bess Marvin."

"So young," murmured the old lady. "Did my relative Sidney Boyd send you? Sidney's the husband of my dear cousin Elsie."

"Are you expecting him today?" Nancy asked.

"This very afternoon!" Mrs Bellhouse said. She motioned for Nancy to bend nearer. "I have something for Sidney, but I don't want that starchy old nurse to know," she said with a chuckle. "See?"

The old lady pulled out a drawer of her night table. Under some tissues lay a pile of currency.

"It's a thousand dollars!" the woman confided.

Nancy pretended surprise. "That's a most generous gift," she remarked.

"No such thing," Mrs Bellhouse answered. "Sidney's selling me stock in a wonderful fur company. The dividends will end my financial worries."

George had posted herself near a front window. When a car parked and a man got out, George gave Nancy a signal and the three girls said a hasty goodbye to Mrs Bellhouse.

In the hall Nancy said quickly, "George, you go downstairs and call the police. Bess and I will hide in the room that connects with the one Mrs Bellhouse is in. It's empty."

The girls retreated just as a man with a pencil-thin moustache strode upstairs and into the woman's room.

"Cousin Clara!" he exclaimed.

Nancy and Bess, watching through a crack in the connecting room, saw Sidney Boyd clasp Mrs Bellhouse's hand. "You look well today. Charming! I wish I were free to spend the afternoon with you. However, I've brought you the stock certificate."

"Sidney, I've been thinking of dear Elsie," Mrs Bellhouse quavered. "She never let me know when she married you."

"I'm sure she did. You've probably forgotten," he said quickly. "Now, before that crabby old nurse comes back—do you have the money?"

"It's right here," said Mrs Bellhouse.

"Fine, Cousin Clara. Here's the stock." He handed her an envelope. "And I'll take the money. Wasn't that easy?"

Nancy and Bess watched indignantly. Then they heard footsteps behind them. It was George, who tip-toed forward and whispered, "Police on the way!"

As Boyd started to leave his victim, he cocked his head and listened. An automobile had just stopped in front of the house. The man looked out a window, then ran from the room.

Nancy followed him as he bolted down the back stair-way. "Come on, girls!" she urged.

The steps were narrow and unlighted. Halfway down, they turned sharply. Here Bess tripped and fell against Nancy, who was just ahead of her.

"Oh," Nancy murmured, grasping for the rail and managing to regain her balance.

George quickly helped Bess to her feet but the delay had given Sidney Boyd a head start. When the girls reached the rear porch of the nursing home, their quarry was nowhere in sight.

"I'm so sorry," Bess said tearfully.

"Never mind," George said, "but you sure were clumsy," she chided.

"Let's separate and look for him," Nancy suggested. George dashed around the east side of the house, while Bess raced towards the rear of the grounds.

Nancy made a beeline for the grove of birches at the west side of the nursing home. She spotted Sidney Boyd crouched behind a clump of saplings.

The man saw her coming. He jumped up and sprinted towards the road. Nancy, still running, cried out loudly, "Help! Help!"

Hearing Nancy's cry, George flagged down the two approaching policemen. "Hurry!" she urged, jumping into their police car. "The thief is down the road, and my friend is chasing him!"

Boyd now crossed the road and started into a field. The officers left their car and sprinted after the swindler. Within seconds the man was a prisoner.

"What's the meaning of this outrage?" he spluttered.

"You'll know fast enough," one of the policemen told him as they walked towards the road where Nancy and George were waiting. "Suppose you listen to this young lady."

"Who's she?" Boyd snapped.

"I'm Nancy Drew," the young sleuth spoke up.

"I've never heard of you," the man said, sneering.

The policemen, the prisoner, Nancy, and George rode back to the nursing home. Bess was waiting at the entrance.

"Nancy, I've been talking with the nurse," she said. "We'd better not tell Mrs Bellhouse about this—the police can give her her money back somehow. If she knew the stock is worthless she might have another attack."

"What do you mean—worthless?" Boyd demanded.

"You know there's no Forest Fur Company," George said, "and Dunstan Lake, Vermont, isn't on the map."

Boyd smiled slyly. "If there's anything phoney about the Forest Fur Company, that's not my fault. I'm merely a broker, and I find this news quite shocking."

"There's a warrant out for your arrest," said one of the policemen. "Let's go!"

The other officer turned to Nancy and said, "I'd like you to follow us."

At the Winchester police station, the captain praised Nancy for her fine detective work. "Miss Drew," he said, taking a piece of paper from his desk, "I think you'll be interested in this. The arresting officers recovered it from Boyd's pocket, along with the thousand dollars he took from the woman in the rest home. It's part of the reason that fellow's behind bars now."

The letter, postmarked New York, read:

*Dear Sid,*
*Tell the boss to come across with some pay or there won't be any more stock printed.*

*Ben*

"That's clear evidence," Nancy said. Returning the paper, she added, "I haven't heard of Ben."

The captain smiled. "We know now that the fur stock is printed in New York and that Boyd is definitely one of the gang. I'll have the New York police trace Ben."

"I'll appreciate it if you'll let me know what comes of this," Nancy said, and wished the captain goodbye. She returned to her car, where Bess and George were waiting.

"At last!" George exclaimed. "You were in there so long we thought we might have to bail you out!"

As Nancy drove towards River Heights, she told her friends what had happened.

"It seems to me this case is pretty well cracked," said George. "Don't you think you need a holiday, Nancy?"

Nancy's eyes twinkled. "Good idea," she said. "How would you like to go to Aunt Eloise's lodge in the Adirondacks? She has a holiday coming up. Maybe she'd come with us—"

"Why, we'd freeze up there!" Bess exclaimed.

"It's between terms at Emerson," Nancy pointed out, ignoring the protest. "We could invite the boys."

The girls began making enthusiastic plans. Suddenly Bess exclaimed, "I'll bet there's something behind this idea of yours. Does it have to do with the fur mystery?"

"Could be," Nancy admitted. "Remember, Aunt Eloise first heard of Dunstan Lake when she was at her summer home. It's possible the gang has headquarters in that vicinity."

"And you want to add detectives Ned Nickerson, Dave Evans, and Burt Eddleton to your investigation squad." George declared.

"Exactly," Nancy admitted. "Suppose you come to my house while I phone Aunt Eloise. I hope we can start day after tomorrow."

Bess looked worried. "What if the boys can't go? It wouldn't be safe up there without some men. The Adirondacks are full of bears."

"Who sleep all winter!" George hooted.

Nancy laughed. "There probably won't be anything more dangerous than a few minks."

"But the stock swindlers—" Bess began.

"No need to worry yet," Nancy advised. "First, I must ask Aunt Eloise if she can go."

# ·13·

## The House Party

NANCY telephoned at once to her aunt. Eloise Drew readily agreed to act as hostess for a house party. "I never dreamed that my clue about Dunstan Lake would bring such an interesting holiday!" she said.

"My hunch may be wrong," Nancy warned. "But we'll have fun, anyway."

"Suppose you pick me up at the station in York Village near camp," her aunt suggested. "I'll arrive there at three-thirty."

Bess and George hung over Nancy's shoulder as she said goodbye, and then made a call to Emerson College. The three boys were enthusiastic about a trip to the Adirondacks. Burt said they could take his family's station wagon.

"Wonderful," said Nancy. "But we'd better have two cars, so I'll take mine, too."

The boys said they could stay only a few days, however, since they had only a short holiday between terms.

This news made Bess pout. When the long-distance conversation was over, she complained, "That's not much time to solve a mystery and have some fun, too!"

Everybody was excited about the excursion to the Adirondacks except Hannah Gruen. The housekeeper worried about possible accidents on the icy roads and a blizzard that might keep them snowbound. "And then you don't know the ways of the woods in the wintertime."

"Hannah," Nancy said, "would you feel happier if someone like John Horn was around to guide us?"

"I certainly would," Hannah answered. "And I'm sure your father would too."

That evening Nancy and Mr Drew went over to call on John Horn, who had just returned from his icefishing trip.

To Nancy's delight, the trapper verified Chuck Wilson's story about his ill-tempered uncle. He told of several incidents which had made him suspicious that the elder Wilson was helping himself to certain funds and not making an accounting of them to the Probate Court.

"But I never could prove it," the trapper said.

"You've been very helpful," the lawyer told him. "And I may call on you to be a witness."

Before the Drews left, Nancy made her request about the trip. The elderly man's eyes glistened.

"You couldn't 'a' asked me anything I'd ruther do," he beamed. "But I won't ride in any of them motor contraptions. No sir-ree. The train for me. And I'll mush in from the station at York. I was brought up on snowshoes."

"Your going relieves my mind," Mr Drew said, and added with a laugh, "Keep my daughter from making any ski jumps after those thieves, will you?"

John Horn chuckled. "Don't you worry. I'll pick up their tracks in the snow and call the police while your daughter's off gallivantin' with the young folks."

Two mornings later the young people began their trip. With skis, sticks, snowshoes, and suitcases in their cars, the girls dressed in colourful ski clothes and the boys in anoraks and fur caps, their group resembled a polar expedition.

"Too bad that old trapper wouldn't let us give him a lift," said Ned as he joined Nancy in the convertible.

"Oh, John Horn's like that. A mind of his own and very independent." Nancy laughed. "When I asked him to help find those swindlers, the old fellow became really excited. Patted his hunting rifle and announced that he intended to snare the varmints!"

For the next three hours everything went well for the travellers. The station wagon followed close behind the convertible. Then, as they reached the foothills of the Adirondacks and began to climb, the roads became icy and the drivers were obliged to decrease their speed to a bare crawl.

Nancy frowned. "I'm worried about Aunt Eloise," she confessed to Ned. "Her train reaches York Village at three-thirty and she's expecting us to pick her up."

"York? That's where we buy the supplies for camp, isn't it?" Ned asked.

"Yes, I'd hoped to get there in time for us to shop before Aunt Eloise arrives."

At that moment a series of loud hoots behind them caused Nancy to slow down and look round. "Oh dear! Burt's car has skidded into a ditch!" She groaned. "We'll have to pull it out."

It took half an hour and considerable huffing and puffing on everybody's part to haul the station wagon back on to the road. When it was once more on its way, Burt realized that the steering gear needed attention.

*"Burt's car has skidded into a ditch!" Nancy cried out*

He signalled to Nancy and drove forward to tell her they must stop at the first town and have it adjusted.

Nancy nodded. "Suppose Ned and I go ahead and leave the food order at the general store. You pick it up. We'll drive Aunt Eloise to camp and start a fire."

Soon the convertible was again on its way. At the store Nancy ordered ham, eggs, bacon, sausages, meat, huge roasting potatoes, bread, fresh fruit, and other necessities.

"Friends of mine will call for the order in a station wagon," Nancy explained to the proprietor.

"Come on. We'd better hurry," Ned warned. "I can hear the train pulling in."

He and Nancy dashed to the station, half expecting to see John Horn alight as well as Eloise Drew. But the trapper was not aboard.

"Hello, Ned!" Miss Drew greeted him, after she embraced her niece. "And where are the rest of my guests?" she inquired.

"They were delayed," said Nancy. "A little trouble with Burt's station wagon. We're to go on ahead."

"I'm glad we're starting at once," Miss Drew observed. "In an hour it will be dark. And that narrow, snowy road leading to my place can be very hazardous."

Nancy and Ned helped Aunt Eloise into the convertible and they began the long climb to the lodge. The road was indeed deep in snow and Ned had to drive very slowly. All were relieved to see the house.

"Look at that snow!" Aunt Eloise exclaimed. "Why, it's halfway up the door."

"Are there any shovels in the garage?" Ned asked as he climbed out of the car.

"I think so," Miss Drew answered.

Ned struggled round the corner of the house to the garage. He came back swinging a shovel and started clearing a path. Soon the station wagon arrived.

"Reinforcements are here," Dave and Burt announced.

In a few minutes they were carrying in the suitcases. The girls and Aunt Eloise followed, shivering in the huge, icy living-room.

"We can soon have some heat," Aunt Eloise said, taking swift charge of the situation. "Boys, there's plenty of wood in the shed outside. Suppose you start a roaring fire in the grate."

"Girls," said Nancy, "let's bring in those groceries from the station wagon."

"Groceries?" Bess gaped.

Nancy's heart sank. "Bess! George!" she gasped. "Didn't you remember to stop for the food? Didn't Burt tell you?"

The blank consternation on her friends' faces was answer enough.

Tired and hungry, the campers had to face it. *There was no food in the house!*

# The Fur Thief

"CHEER UP!" Aunt Eloise encouraged her guests. "The situation isn't too black. I left a few cans in the pantry here. If you don't object to beans—"

"Beans! Oh, welcome word!" cried Bess, rolling her eyes ecstatically. "I'm ravenous enough to eat tacks."

"Then you'll have to earn your supper," George said firmly. "Get a mop. This place must be cleaned before we eat."

In the midst of their tidying the lodge a knock came on the door. John Horn walked in. The old fellow looked ruddy and fit after his trek on snowshoes. He explained that he had come up the day before and was camping out in the hills Indian style. When they told him of their predicament about food, he looked amused.

"Shucks, nobody here need go hungry." He chuckled. "I shot some rabbits on the way. I'll bring 'em in and give you folks a real treat!"

After consuming the nourishing beans and John Horn's delicious rabbit, cooked on a spit in the fireplace, everyone felt satisfied and content. Then, gathering around him, Aunt Eloise and her guests listened for two hours to the old trapper's yarns. Later, when Nancy asked him if he had found out anything about Dunstan Lake, he shook his head.

"Nope. Nobody I met ever heard of the man, Nancy.

Nor of that Forest Fur Company, either. But they say there's three mink ranches around here owned by outside folks."

Suddenly Eloise Drew snapped her fingers. "I just recalled that I heard the name Dunstan Lake twice. The second time was last summer at the Longview Inn five miles from here. I was leaving the dining-room when I overheard a woman mention the name."

"Maybe it's another clue," Nancy spoke up. "I think I'll go over there right after breakfast tomorrow and speak to the manager. I'd like to hike over. Could I make it on snowshoes, Mr Horn?"

"Oh, sure—that is, if you got good muscles, and you look as if you do. Well, folks," the trapper said, rising, "I'll be on my way."

He would not accept a bunk with the boys and went off whistling in the darkness. The house party guests rolled wearily into bed and slept soundly.

Next morning the prospect of a second meal of beans for breakfast had little appeal for the campers. At Nancy's suggestion the young people tramped down to the frozen lake, resolved to try some ice fishing.

The boys hacked a hole in the ice fifty feet from shore and carefully lowered several lines with baited hooks. But although they waited patiently, there was not a bite.

"I guess we'll eat beans—and like it," George groaned.

"Hal-loo there! What you doin'? Lookin' for a walrus?" called a voice from the shore.

They turned to see John Horn standing there with a heavy pack on his back. The old trapper explained that he had risen before daylight and gone down to York Village.

"I brought your grub." He grinned. "Wanta eat?"

"Do we!" cried Burt, dropping the line he was holding. "I'll swap an uncaught fish for a stack of hot-dogs any day!"

The others echoed his sentiments as they rushed to join the trapper and relieve him of the food.

Directly after breakfast Nancy and Ned fastened snowshoes to their hiking boots and set out for Long-view Inn. The snow was crisp and just hard enough for firm going. Shortly before noon they arrived at the entrance to the big resort hotel.

"What a grand spot for winter sports!" Nancy exclaimed. She gazed admiringly at the high ski jump and the numerous ski trails and toboggan slides.

"Sure is." Ned nodded. "I wish we had time to try 'em. But I suppose you want to find out about Dunstan Lake. Well, where do we begin our investigations?"

"Pardon me. But would you two be interested in purchasing tickets to our charity contest? a strange voice inquired.

The couple looked round to face a smiling elderly woman. She went on to explain that the tickets were for a skiing party the next afternoon, to be followed by a trapper's dinner at the inn.

Ned was just about to say that they could not make it, when Nancy surprised him by telling the woman they would take seven tickets! Ned dug into his pocket for the money.

But as they entered the hotel, he asked, "Nancy, why did you do that?"

"Sorry, Ned, I'll pay for the tickets."

"That's all right, Nancy, but maybe the others won't want to go."

"I was thinking of Mitzi Channing," Nancy said. "If she's in the neighbourhood, she might show up."

"You're right. Well, let's call on the manager."

Mr Pike had been with the inn for five years, but he had never heard of a Dunstan Lake, nor anyone named Channing. He promised, however, to make inquiries among the guests and to let Nancy know.

When they left the hotel, Ned said eagerly, "Let's go over and look at that Olympic ski jump."

The jump was truly spectacular and near the base of it was a skating pond. At the edge of the ice stood two mammoth figures which had been carved out of snow.

"Aren't they wonderful!" Nancy cried out.

As she and Ned stood staring at the snow giants, Nancy felt a hand on her arm.

"Nancy Drew—this *is* a surprise!" said a familiar voice.

"Why, Chuck Wilson!" Nancy gasped. "What are you doing here?"

Working as a ski instructor." Chuck grinned. "The regular pro has a broken leg. And now tell me what you're doing here."

Nancy introduced the two young men, then told Chuck about the house party at her aunt's camp.

"Oh, Chuck, I have a grand surprise for you!" she added. "Guess what! John Horn's here!"

"Here!" The skier looked incredulous. "At your camp? I'll be right over!"

Ned looked none too pleased at this suggestion. "John's not staying with us," he said.

Ned lost his glum look, however, when Chuck insisted upon lending the couple skis, boots and sticks, and suggested that they take a few runs. For the next half hour Ned and Nancy enjoyed themselves on the ski slopes.

"Nancy, your skiing has certainly improved," Ned said, smiling.

"The credit for that goes to Chuck."

Below them, Chuck Wilson waved his hand. "Hey, why don't you try jumping off that mogul?" he called.

"I'm game," Nancy cried, pushing off, after leaving her sticks against a tree. "Come on, Ned!"

Nancy went first, taking off beautifully from the top of the huge bump. Ned followed but his was by far the higher and the longer jump.

"Well, at least I didn't spill." Nancy laughed as they pulled up alongside the ski instructor. "And now I think we'd better start back to camp."

"Nancy, I'll see you again soon, won't I?" Chuck pleaded.

"We're all coming over here tomorrow," she promised. Then, with a teasing glance at Ned, she added, "But there's no reason why we can't see more of each other today. Ned and I haven't had lunch, so why don't you join us in the dining-room?"

"Thanks, I will. But let's go downstairs to the snack corner."

Nancy and Ned returned the borrowed equipment, and Chuck checked his skis and sticks at the long rack outside the beam-ceilinged room, which was crowded with skiing enthusiasts.

Their appetites whetted by a morning in the crisp mountain air, the trio ate heartily. When they finished, Ned and Nancy insisted they must leave, instead of joining the group which lingered by the fireplace discussing slalom and downhill racing.

Outside, as they were fastening on their snowshoes for the long hike back to camp, Nancy turned to Chuck. "By the way, do you know of any mink ranches around here?"

"There's one up on that ridge where the run for the ski jump starts. The ranch is owned by Charlie Wells."

"Let's go home that way," Nancy suggested to Ned. "We may pick up some information about the Forest Fur Company and Dunstan Lake."

They rode up on the lift and trekked off along the ridge. Half a mile further on, they neared the ranch buildings. A man came running towards them.

"Did you meet anyone or see anyone leaving here?" he asked excitedly.

"No," Ned replied. "Is something the matter?"

"I'll say there's something the matter," the man growled. "Some of my finest mink pelts have been stolen!"

# ·15·

## *Racing a Storm*

STOLEN!

An idea clicked in Nancy's mind. Could the person who had taken the pelts from Wells's ranch be one of the Forest Fur Company gang? Quickly she introduced Ned and herself.

"Did you lose many minks?" Nancy asked.

"About two thousand dollars' worth," the man replied. "Half my take for the year."

"You own the mink ranch?" Ned inquired.

"Yes. I'm Charlie Wells."

"When were the pelts stolen?"

"I'm not sure. Just a few minutes ago I noticed the door of the storage house was half open."

"Did you see any new tracks in the snow?" Nancy asked.

"No, but we had a hard blow here early this morning. The snow could have filled up the tracks."

"Perhaps the furs were taken last night," Nancy commented. "A thief wouldn't dare prowl around in the daylight. May we see where you kept the pelts, Mr Wells?"

"Certainly." He led them to a small building attached to the back of the house.

As they approached the door, Ned remarked, "I

notice only one set of footprints here, and they must be yours, Mr Wells."

Nancy stooped down. With her glove she lightly brushed away some of the powder snow. Another man's prints were visible in the crust underneath the recently blown powder. "I wish we could follow these tracks," Nancy said.

"You're not going to try brushing away all this snow!" Ned exclaimed.

Nancy smiled. "If I thought it would lead us to the thief, I'd try it."

"I'm afraid my pelts are in another state by this time," Mr Wells said mournfully.

"Maybe we can help you get them back," Nancy suggested. "Have you ever heard of the Forest Fur Company? Or Mr and Mrs R. I. Channing? Or Dunstan Lake?"

At each question Mr Wells shook his head.

"Have you notified the police about the theft?" Nancy asked.

"No."

"I'll do it for you," she offered.

The rancher led them into his small house, which was furnished with rustic pieces. A large deer head hung over the living-room fireplace.

Nancy telephoned the State Police. She reported the theft at the Wells Ranch and then told about the stock swindle and the arrest of Boyd.

"I believe a man named Channing may know something about this theft," she said.

The officer was grateful for the information and said, "We'll follow up your lead right away!"

When Nancy returned from the telephone, she found

Mr Wells pointing to the deer head and telling Ned how he had shot the animal in the nearby woods.

Ned was impressed. "I'd like to shoot one and hang the head in our fraternity house!"

The ranch owner winked at Nancy. "It's all yours, son, if Miss Drew nabs the fur thief."

"I'll do my best," the young detective promised. "Mr Wells, this is my first chance to see a mink ranch. May Ned and I look around a bit?"

"I'll go with you," the rancher replied. As they stepped outside, he glanced at the low, dark clouds rolling in from the north. "More snow on the way," he predicted.

"Then we mustn't stay long," Ned said.

Mr Wells led them to one of several small, shed-like buildings set back some distance from the house. The shed was about six feet wide and had separate pens on either side of a central aisle. Some fifty glossy little animals occupied the pens.

"They're beautiful," Nancy remarked. "But they must require a lot of care."

Mr Wells shook his head. "All they need is the right kind of food and a clean, cool place where there isn't too much sunlight."

"Sounds like a good business," Ned said.

"It is, for an outdoor man," the rancher replied. "If you want to establish a mink farm, you should start with the finest, healthiest animals you can buy. Then get settled in a cold climate—makes the fur grow thick. In this country you find most of the mink ranches in Maine, Vermont, New Hampshire, Massachusetts, and northern New York."

"What do minks eat?" Nancy asked.

"A mink likes lean meat and fish best," Mr Wells said enthusiastically. "But he'll eat table scraps, vegetables—even field mice. Wild minks are fierce little fighters and very cunning."

"Very interesting," said Ned. "Now we'd better leave. We want to get home ahead of the storm."

As they left the building, Nancy suddenly spied a small, dark object half hidden under the snow. "The thief may have dropped this!" she thought excitedly.

The rancher, walking ahead of the couple, did not see Nancy run over to the spot, stoop down, and reach for the object. Suddenly Ned cried, "Don't touch that!"

He gave Nancy a shove which sent her reeling away from the object.

"Ned, what—"

"It's a trap, Nancy!"

Mr Wells turned and hurried back to them. "That's a fox trap!" he warned. "I keep them all around the grounds to catch foxes who try to raid the mink pens."

"Thanks, Ned," Nancy said. "I'm glad you recognized it."

The young people said goodbye to Mr Wells and started off. "Hurry!" Ned urged. "I don't like the look of that sky."

"Let's go along behind the mink sheds," Nancy suggested. "The thieves may have left clues."

"Okay."

Behind the sheds a thick row of evergreens marked the Wells property line. Nancy and Ned followed it, scanning the ground hopefully.

Once Ned happened to look up. Near him, hanging from a shoulder-high branch, was a strand of white yarn. "Here's something!" he exclaimed.

Nancy plodded over. "Well, Mr Detective, what's your theory?"

"Anyone trying to keep out of sight against the snow would wear white," Ned said. "Maybe our man snagged his shoulder or sleeve on these trees as he approached the mink pens."

"How right you are," said Nancy. "Let's see if we can find more of that yarn."

The two followed the line of evergreens into dense woods. From time to time, wisps of white wool on tree branches marked a clear trail.

But soon the woods gave way to open ground, dotted with knee-high clumps of berry bushes. A brisk wind hit Nancy and Ned with full force as they emerged into the open. The cold stung their faces.

"We'd better make for camp in a hurry," Nancy said. "We'll retrace our steps."

They turned, then stopped. The wind had blown snow over their tracks.

"Seems to me we came from over that way," Nancy said, trying to sound cheerful.

Ned nodded. "Let's go! And make it fast!"

Neither spoke as they tramped along. The daylight grew dimmer. For two hours they trudged ahead through the snow.

Finally Nancy called, "Ned! We should have reached camp long ago."

"I know that," the youth said grimly. "I don't want to worry you, Nancy, but I'm afraid we're lost!"

# ·16·

## An SOS

FOR several seconds neither Nancy nor Ned spoke. Each was trying to figure out how to get back to the lodge before the storm.

Ned sheltered his eyes with one hand and peered through the rapidly falling dusk. All he could distinguish at first were rolling stretches of snow-covered landscape. The lost couple might have been in the arctic wastelands. Then Ned spied a lean-to and they hiked to it.

"Wood!" he exclaimed, seeing a pile of logs in one corner. "I'm going to build a fire. That may attract someone's attention."

"And we can eat," said Nancy. "I have two chocolate bars in my pocket."

The crackling fire and the chocolate revived their spirits, though no one came to guide them out of the snowy wilderness. Finally, when the fire died down, they set off again. Their way lay downhill, which at this moment seemed the easiest to take.

"I have a pocket torch," said Nancy. "I'll blink an SOS. Three short, three long, then three short. Right?"

"Right," Ned agreed.

Nancy clicked the signal several times as they crunched along. Again they had just about given up hope of help, and were floundering in a snowbank, when Ned said:

"Listen! I thought I heard a shout."

Nancy glanced quickly over her shoulder. "You're right!" she cried. "There *is* a man over there. John Horn!"

The trapper came plunging towards them through a drift. "I saw your distress signal, folks!" he yelled. "You lost? Why, Nancy! Ned!"

When Ned explained that they were indeed lost, the old man looked hurt. "You shoulda asked me to guide you," he reproached them. "But anyway, I can show you a short cut through the woods. You can make it home before it snows."

"You're certainly a lifesaver," Nancy said gratefully. "As a reward, I'll tell you some good news. Chuck Wilson is staying at the inn. We saw him this afternoon."

"You don't say!" Horn exclaimed, his leathery face spreading into a delighted grin. "Well, I'll sure have to tramp over there in a hurry and visit the boy."

He started off, with Nancy following and Ned bringing up the rear. Presently Nancy noticed that the trapper had about a dozen beautiful mink pelts strapped to his knapsack. She admired them, then asked where they had come from.

"Oh, I picked 'em up," John Horn answered vaguely. "They're the best mink there is!"

Nancy frowned worriedly as she tramped silently behind the trapper. Twenty minutes later they came to a well-defined trail, marked with the stompings of many feet.

"Just follow this," said their guide, "and you'll come

to your camp. So long, I'll drop over tomorrow."

As the couple watched their rescuer's sturdy figure vanish into the night, Ned said, "Nancy, you look upset. Surely you're not afraid we'll get lost again?"

"No, it's not that," she replied. "I was wondering about those valuable pelts John Horn was carrying, and the ones that were stolen from Mr Wells."

"Good grief! You don't think that old man's a thief, do you?" Ned demanded.

"I hate to think that," Nancy admitted. "He could have set a lot of traps, I suppose, and had some luck."

Ned shrugged, then said if Horn had stolen the pelts, more than likely he would have hidden them.

Nancy agreed, saying, "I guess I'm so tired and hungry that my suspicions are getting the better of me."

The trail led almost directly to the back of the lodge. "We were going in circles," Ned remarked ruefully, "before John Horn found us." As they climbed the porch steps, snow began to fall.

They were welcomed by a frantic group. Aunt Eloise had been chiding herself for letting the couple go off without a guide, and actually wept with joy to see her niece and Ned.

Again they all enjoyed supper before a blazing fire, while Nancy and Ned recounted their adventures. The prospect of attending the big ski party at the hotel aroused the young people's enthusiasm. They agreed to follow Aunt Eloise's advice and retire early in preparation for the big day.

Nancy was so weary that she tumbled into bed like a rag doll. It seemed as if her head had barely touched the pillow when she heard her aunt's voice.

"Nancy! Wake up!" Miss Drew urged. "It's a lovely,

sunny day. And there's a telegram for you, dear. A boy just brought it from the village."

"Read it to me, please," mumbled sleepy Nancy.

"Very well." Her aunt hurriedly slit the envelope and scanned the teletyped lines. Then she read the message aloud: " 'Nancy, phone me from Longview Inn. Love, Father.' "

"Aunt Eloise, I don't understand," Nancy said, now fully awake and sitting up in bed. "Why should Dad send me a telegram like that?"

"Perhaps he has learned something that will help solve this fur mystery," her aunt suggested.

"Perhaps. But why should Dad ask me to phone from the hotel instead of the village? And why would he sign the message 'Father' instead of 'Dad' as he always does? Aunt Eloise, it looks as if that telegram might be a fake."

"Oh dear!" said Aunt Eloise. "Those thieves have probably found out you're here. Well, that settles it. No more trips except in a group. And I'm going to phone your father myself from the village."

When Nancy entered the living-room a short time later, she found George and the three boys busily waxing their skis. "We've decided to go to the party on skis," Ned explained. "The snow's just right, and we'll work up a better appetite for that trapper's dinner." He grinned.

"Dinner?" Nancy asked. "How about breakfast?"

"We've eaten, sleepyhead," George replied.

Nancy prepared bacon, eggs, and toast for herself. She had just finished eating when Bess came running in, her cheeks flushed with excitement.

"Listen, everybody!" she cried out. "Someone's been

snooping around this house! I saw a lot of strange tracks."

The others rushed outside. In the new-fallen snow there were indeed a series of footprints encircling the house. A man had been both peering and eavesdropping!

The young people trailed the tracks away from the lodge and on down to the edge of a small grove. Here they disappeared as mysteriously as they had begun.

Where had the eavesdropper gone and who was he?

Back at the lodge, an ugly possibility came to Aunt Eloise's mind. The gang of fur thieves and stock swindlers had learned of Boyd's arrest and wanted to get revenge on Nancy! Also, they would stop at nothing to keep her from tracking them down.

Miss Drew felt the responsibility for her niece's safety weighing heavily on her. Nancy must be protected. It might be only a matter of time before the mysterious eavesdropper would return, not to observe, but to strike!

# ·17·

## The Hidden Cabin

DISAPPOINTED not to have found any trace of the eaves-dropper, the boys and girls returned to Eloise Drew's lodge and made plans to go to Longview Inn.

"I'm driving to the village with Aunt Eloise," announced Bess. "We'll meet you at the hotel for lunch."

The teacher recommended that the others start out at once. "It will take you until noon to reach the inn," she reminded them.

Just as the hikers were about to set off, John Horn strode up with a telegram.

"Did you get one of these this morning, Nancy?" he asked. "Woman at the telegraph office in the village sent a boy out with one, but he didn't come back there and they wondered if he delivered it."

"Yes, he did," said Nancy. The telegram proved to be a duplicate of the one she had received.

Nancy told John Horn about the mysterious eaves-dropper. "Would you look at the spot where the tracks end and see what you think? His tracks simply vanish."

The trapper followed Nancy to the place. He chuckled. "The fellow used the old Injun method of covering his tracks," he declared. "Walked backward and brushed the prints away with a broom he'd made of an evergreen bough. He wouldn't keep that up for long, though. Maybe we'll pick up the tracks some distance on. I'll go with you."

Nancy went back for her skis, then the group set off for the inn, watching carefully for footprints.

"Hey, gang!" Dave called suddenly. "Look at the circle of ski tracks just ahead."

"How odd!" said Ned. "It looks as if two or three people met here and—"

"And had a conference," Nancy finished. "I'll bet that evesdropper has skis! The tracks seem to lead away in three directions—so why don't we separate and see where they go?"

Burt grinned. "Give us our orders, ma'am!"

"Okay. Dave, will you follow the tracks that lead towards the hotel? Tell Aunt Eloise and Bess that the rest of us may be delayed. George and Burt, will you swing right towards the Wells Ranch?" She pointed.

"Okay!" said Burt.

"Ned and I will take that left trail into the woods," Nancy went on. "Mr Horn, will you come with us?" As he nodded, she said, "If any of you find our eavesdropper, try to nab him!"

When Nancy's group started off, John Horn said, "I know one thing you'll find. There's a cabin ahead of us that don't seem natural."

"How do you mean?" Ned asked.

"Nobody there, and it's locked tight and boarded at the windows. The right kind o' woods people always keep their cabins open for other hunters to use."

The three searchers followed the ski tracks until they disappeared about a hundred feet beyond the cab n the trapper described. Their quarry evidently had removed his skis and continued on foot.

"His footprints aren't like the ones the eavesdropper left at Aunt Eloise's cabin," Nancy remarked, "so we'd better turn back."

The trio stopped first to inspect the small cabin which was locked. At the door were lots of footprints.

"I wonder if they were made by hikers who stopped here to rest," Nancy said.

"Or by men who stay here," Ned replied. "By the way, that padlock hasn't been on the door long. It's brand new!"

John Horn nodded. "Reckon I won't go to the hotel yet. I'll just stay here and scout around a bit. You folks run along."

Nancy and Ned reached the Longview Inn about twenty minutes later. It was crowded with sports enthusiasts. George and Burt hurried across the lobby to meet them, and reported that neither they nor Dave had found anything of consequence.

Aunt Eloise beckoned her niece aside. "Your father and I are worried, Nancy," she said. "I talked with him on the telephone. He didn't send that telegram!"

"I wonder who did," Nancy mused.

"Someone who wanted to make sure you would be at the inn today," her aunt declared. "You will be extra careful, won't you?"

"Of course," Nancy promised. "But there's not much danger with so many friends around."

Although she pretended to take her aunt's news lightly, Nancy was aware that the telegram might indicate trouble. "The Channings must know by now that I'm responsible for Boyd's arrest," she thought. "They may try to trap me!"

Aunt Eloise continued to worry during lunch, and

ate very little. Chuck Wilson appeared while they were finishing dessert, and Nancy introduced him to her aunt and the others.

A short time later a bugle announced the opening of the afternoon programme. Everyone hurried outside to watch or participate in the contests.

"To start the afternoon's events," the master of ceremonies said, "the management is proud to present a special feature. Chuck Wilson, our new ski instructor, will make an exhibition jump from Big Hill."

There was a murmur of anticipation from the spectators as all eyes turned to the top of the slope where the blonde young man stood poised for the start. At a blast from the bugle, he was off.

Chuck raced down the incline, then soared into space, his arms spread out like a great bird's wings. For an instant he seemed to hang in the sunlit sky. A moment later he came swooping gracefully to earth.

The crowd burst into applause and Burt declared with a grin, "I'd give up college if I thought I could learn to do that!"

As he and the others skied over to congratulate Chuck, Nancy scanned the crowd of spectators. The Channings did not seem to be present.

Aunt Eloise came to her niece's side and spoke in a low voice. "I hope you're not planning to enter any of the events, dear," she said. "Your enemies may be waiting for your name to be announced."

Nancy agreed. She took off her skis and went to explain her decision to Ned. The young man was disappointed but said, "The important thing is to keep you safe, Nancy. Okay if I find another partner to enter the next event?"

"Of course," said Nancy. A few minutes later she watched as Ned and a pretty girl joined in the two-legged race.

Nancy left her aunt's side and pushed her way among the milling groups. She still saw no sign of the couple who had taken part in the stock swindles. "I'm wrong about their being here," she decided finally. "I should have entered the games after all. Hunches aren't—"

"Psst! Nancy!"

The urgent voice came from behind her. She whirled to face John Horn. The old man's eyes sparkled with excitement.

He beckoned with a calloused finger. "Follow me!"

# ·18·

## *A Weird Light*

Nancy looked anxiously about in hopes of seeing either Ned or one of her other friends. But none of them was in sight. John Horn tugged impatiently at her coat sleeve.

"I tell you we got to hurry, Nancy," he pleaded. "She's over on that pond in the woods right now. And skatin' around bold as you please!"

"Who's skating?" Nancy demanded.

"Why, that woman who sold me the fake fur stock," the old trapper snorted. "That thievin' Mrs Channing, of course!"

At the name Channing, Nancy hesitated no longer. "Lead the way!" she urged.

An instant later the two were running across the hotel grounds. They headed into the woods at the rear of the inn and trudged through the snow for nearly a quarter of a mile.

"There she is!" Horn pointed out. They slowed down and cautiously approached a small, cleared pond.

Nancy felt a tingle of excitement run down her spine. She stood on tiptoe for a better view and craned her neck. As Mitzi Adele ended a series of figures, she was facing Nancy directly.

The tall, slender brunette suddenly realized she had

*"Fool!" said John Horn. "She'll break an ankle!"*

been discovered. Like a flash she shot back towards the far bank. Without removing her skates, she raced off among the trees.

"Fool!" said John Horn. "She'll break an ankle!"

He was already taking snowshoes from his back, and quickly fastened them on to his boots.

"Looks like it's goin' to be a race!" he observed. "You follow as fast as you can, Nancy."

He soon outdistanced Nancy, who had tried sliding across the ice to save time. But she had fallen twice and wasted precious minutes.

Some distance ahead, the trapper saw Mitzi. She was seated on a log and had just finished changing into hiking boots. She leaped to her feet and fled further into the woods, but the old trapper was gaining with every step.

Nancy found their trail and sped after them as fast as she could through the deep snow. Suddenly she heard a scream, followed by:

"Let me go!"

A moment later she came in view of Mitzi and the trapper. The woman was kicking and scratching John Horn as he held her firmly by one arm. Mitzi's eyes blazed with anger.

"I'll have you arrested for this!" she panted.

"Oh, no, you won't, Mrs Channing," called Nancy, running up. "We're going to turn *you* over to the police."

Mitzi glared. "Why, if it isn't little Miss Detective herself!" she sneered. "And what have I done?"

"A great deal, Mitzi Channing. You've been selling fake stock certificates and you've stolen furs and jewellery. That should be enough."

"That stock is perfectly good," Mitzi snapped. "And I've never stolen anything. If this big gorilla will just —let—go—!" she added, trying to twist away from the trapper's grasp.

"Where's your husband?" Nancy demanded. "And where's Dunstan Lake?"

"*Wh-at?*"

The startled woman flung back her head. As she did so, her cap, loosened by her struggles, fell to the ground, disclosing a pair of sparkling earrings. They were shaped like small arrows with diamonds at each tip.

"Those are Mrs Packer's stolen earrings," Nancy charged.

"They are not. They're mine," Mitzi retorted. Then suddenly she clamped her lips tightly together and refused to say another word.

"Nancy, there's a couple of state troopers at the hotel," said John Horn. "If you'll hurry back and get 'em, I'll march our prisoner along and meet you halfway."

"I'll bring them as fast as I can," Nancy promised, and started off at a run.

She planned to tell her aunt and the others about the capture, but met the troopers first and decided to wait until the prisoner was in custody. She told her story quickly and led the officers towards the spot where she had left the captive and John Horn.

But when they arrived, there was no sign of Mitzi Channing. They saw only the limp body of John Horn, lying unconscious on the snow with a large welt behind one ear.

"Oh!" Nancy cried in horror, and knelt beside him. One of the troopers reached into his pocket for a tiny phial, removed the cap, and held the spirits of ammonia under John Horn's nose. Meanwhile, the other officer was inspecting the ground. He said that what had happened was plain. Footprints indicated that the trapper had been overpowered by two large men. Mitzi had vanished into the woods with her rescuers.

Fortunately, John Horn was not badly hurt and revived within a few minutes. He explained that he had been jumped from behind and had not seen his attackers.

"But I think I can identify one of those men," Nancy told the troopers. "He is named Channing, alias Jacques Fremont."

One trooper immediately set out to trail the men, while his partner hastened off to dispatch a radio alarm. Nancy and John Horn walked slowly back to the inn.

The old man protested that he was all right and that he needed no coddling. But Nancy insisted that he take a room at the hotel and have the house physician examine his injured head.

Nancy's aunt and her young friends were greatly upset by the incident. They concluded that the Forest Fur Company gang must be desperate. Nancy called State Police headquarters, but there was no word about Mitzi or the men.

Chuck Wilson was deeply concerned about his old friend and spent nearly an hour in John Horn's room. Because of this, he almost missed the special trapper's dinner which the guests enjoyed immensely. The management had provided a hillbilly orchestra, which played old-time ballads and lively polkas. Afterwards, the tables and chairs were cleared away for a series of square dances.

Nancy swung gaily through the "grand right and left," then promenaded with Ned as her partner. When it was over, Chuck Wilson came to join them.

"I'm going upstairs again to see how old John is feeling," he said. "Do you folks want to come?"

"Oh yes," Nancy answered.

They found the trapper pacing the floor of his room like a caged bear. "The Doc won't let me git outta here till mornin'," he grumbled. "He must think I'm a softy."

"Nothing of the sort," Nancy replied, and added affectionately, "You probably saved my life, Mr Horn. If I'd been standing guard over Mitzi, those men might have carried me off and dropped me down some snowy ravine."

"Don't talk like that!" Ned said severely.

While she had been talking, Nancy had walked to a window to gaze at the beautiful moonlit landscape. Suddenly her attention was caught by a glimmer of light along the ridge at the top of Big Hill. A moment later she could see the steady beam of a flashlight moving rapidly towards the ski run. It seemed very strange at this hour.

"Boys," she called, "why would anyone be up near the top of the jump at night?"

"I can't imagine," said Chuck as he and Ned joined her at the window. "Come on! Let's find out!"

The three young people waved a quick goodbye to the trapper and hurried downstairs to the cloakrooms. Hastily changing to ski clothes, they dashed outdoors.

For a moment there was no sign of the light. Then suddenly it showed up again at the top of the ski run and came hurtling downward, as the unknown jumper soared expertly at the take-off and landed below with a soft swish and a thud.

"Good grief!" Chuck cried. "What a chance he took! Let's speak to him!"

He and Ned raced off into the darkness, for already the light had disappeared and a cloud had cut off the moonlight.

Nancy waited until the cloud passed over, then tried to spot the jumper. She could not see him.

"Where could he have gone?" she asked herself. "That man wasn't just a phantom. He was flesh and blood!"

She turned towards the lake and the two giant snow statues which marked the end of the ski jump. Nancy's heart pounded at the sight she saw.

By a mere flicker of light that glowed, then vanished like a firefly, she could detect the shadowy outline of a crouching figure in a white sweater huddled behind the nearer statue. The person was cramming a bulky pouch into a hollow of the snowman!

As Nancy opened her mouth to call Chuck and Ned, a rough hand was clapped over her face.

"Quiet!" a harsh voice commanded. "*And don't try to run away or you'll get hurt!*"

# · 19 ·

## *Zero Hour*

THERE was no escaping from the man's iron grasp. With her captor's fingers firmly gripping both arms, Nancy stood helpless, while the other man ran over from the statue. Roughly he stuffed a handkerchief into her mouth, tied her hands behind her, and bound her ankles together. Then the two men carried her swiftly towards the woods.

"If only Ned or Chuck had seen me!" Nancy thought. "Here I am with friends so close by and I can't even call for aid."

Although Nancy could not see the men's faces, in a few minutes she knew who her abductors were, for they began to talk freely.

"Say, Jacques, how much further is it to that cabin?" the shorter of the pair asked.

*Jacques Fremont!* The man whose other name was Channing! The man at the skating exhibition in Montreal! If only the police had not been forced to release him!"

"Just a little ways, Lake," he replied.

Nancy caught her breath. So Dunstan Lake was a man, not a place;

Channing gave a sardonic laugh. "All we need to do

is dump the Drew girl inside and lock the door. The place probably won't be opened again until summer."

"What a relief to have her out of the way!" growled his companion. "We had an airtight racket until Miss Detective began snooping around, asking for the Channings and Dunstan Lake. Although how she found out where we were, I'll never know."

"She's clever," Channing admitted. "But too clever for her own good. Now Miss Nancy Drew is going to pay for her smartness.

"Well, Lake, here we are. Suppose we see if this girl detective can solve the mystery of the locked cabin with both her hands and feet tied," Channing continued with a harsh laugh.

The cabin was bitterly cold, even worse than out-doors, Nancy thought, as her abductors flung her down on a bare bunk. Then, in the glare of a flashlight, Dunstan Lake, a squarish man with a bulldog face and beady eyes, made a mocking bow.

"Goodbye, Miss Drew." He smirked. "Happy sleuthing!"

"Come along! Let's get out of here," Channing snapped impatiently. "It's time we picked up Mitzi at the camp. She'll be tired of waiting."

Nancy shivered and closed her eyes despairingly as she heard the door slam and the padlock snap. She struggled to get out of her bonds, but it was useless. Already her fingers were becoming cold. With every passing minute the cabin grew more frigid. Nancy wondered desperately how long she could survive.

She knew that her only hope lay in exercise. She raised and lowered her bound ankles as high as she could until she was puffing with exhaustion. As she rested a moment, the fearful cold took possession of her again.

Nancy decided to try rolling on the floor. She managed to get off the bunk, and in doing so loosened the gag in her mouth. Crying loudly for help, she waited hopefully for an answer. None came.

She rolled, twisted, and yelled until she was bruised and hoarse. Finally her voice gave out completely. Her strength was gone. She became drowsy, and knew what this meant. Her body was succumbing to the below-freezing temperature!

Meanwhile, back at the slope, Ned and Chuck had completed a futile search for the mysterious jumper and were now walking to the spot where they had left Nancy. "I can't figure out why that fellow took off at night," said Chuck. "He could be arrested, you know. It's against all regulations."

"It was probably some crackpot who wanted to prove how brave he is." Ned shrugged. "Say, Nancy's gone!"

"I wouldn't worry." Chuck smiled. "She probably was chilled and went back to the hotel."

"Not Nancy!" Ned retorted. "She never gives up! If Nancy's not here, it's for a good reason. She probably spotted one of those swindlers she's been looking for and is trailing him alone!"

Nevertheless, Chuck persuaded Ned to go back to the hotel to look for Nancy. She had not come in, Bess reported. "What's going on?"

"Tell you later," Ned called as he and Chuck dashed off.

When they reached the ski slope, Chuck cried out, "Look, somebody's coming down Big Hill again! Two men with flashlights."

"But those fellows are descending like sane men," Ned observed. "They aren't taking any jumps."

The newcomers were state troopers. They said they were searching for the thief who again had stolen some mink pelts from the Wells Ranch. Chuck told them about the foolhardy jumper and they shook their heads in disgust. The men were about to go on when Ned stopped them.

"Have you seen a girl in a ski outfit?" he asked. "She was out here with us when we were looking for that crazy skier. Now she has disappeared and I'm afraid she's trailing the same thieves you are."

"Thieves?" the troopers echoed.

"Yes, thieves," Ned went on. "The girl is Nancy Drew, the one who captured that swindler, Mitzi Channing, this afternoon. But the woman got away."

"I heard about that over the police radio," one of the men said. "We'd better help you hunt for your friend. She may be in danger."

"We haven't much chance of trailing anyone," the other remarked. "There's been such a crowd around here, the place is full of tracks. How long has it been since you saw the young lady?"

"About twenty minutes," Chuck answered.

"Then she can't be far away," said the younger trooper. "Why not divide our forces so as to cover as much territory as possible?"

It was quickly agreed among the four that Chuck would search the hotel grounds while Ned followed the shoreline along the lake. The two troopers would examine the surrounding woods.

"Let's arrange a signal," said one of them. "The first man to find the girl will turn the beam of his torch towards the sky and wave it in an arc. In case of emergency, he will blink the light rapidly until help arrives. Is that clear?"

"Perfectly," Ned said impatiently. "Let's go!"

The next hour was torture for the searchers. The heavy snow made the going difficult, and a keen, arctic wind developed that knifed through their stout woollen clothing and sent the tears down their smarting cheeks. Added to this, their spirits were becoming low.

At the end of the hour the four met. No one had found a trace of Nancy. The troopers went back to their headquarters to report, while the two boys returned to the hotel. A frantic Aunt Eloise and the remainder of her house party rushed to meet them at the door.

"Where's Nancy?" Miss Drew demanded. "When none of you came back for the dancing, we all became worried and tried to find out what happened. But nobody knows a thing."

The two boys told the story of the strange skier and their separation from Nancy. Everyone listened in shocked silence. Then Bess offered a ray of hope.

"If John Horn is still upstairs, why don't we get his advice?" she suggested. "He knows more about the woods than all of us."

"Say, that's a great idea," Chuck agreed, rushing to the stairway. I'll ask the old fellow—" The rest was lost as he bounded up the steps.

In a few minutes he was back. With him was John Horn. The bandage on the old trapper's head was awry. He looked pale, but he insisted upon joining them in a new search.

"If those swindlers nabbed Nancy Drew, they wouldn't 'a' dared take her far off," he said. "I'll bet they took her to that empty cabin in the woods. Yes, sir. That's where they've left her. It's the only place around here where they could hide her without bein' found out."

"Oh, why didn't I think of that?" Ned chided himself, starting for the door. "If anything happens to Nancy—"

"Hold on!" Dave objected. "Burt and I are fresher and we can strike out faster. George and Bess can follow us with a Thermos flask of hot coffee and a blanket. But you and Chuck are in no shape to go."

"What do you mean?" Ned glared. "Maybe I can't go as fast as you, but what if there's trouble? I want to be there to help!"

"So do I," Chuck said firmly.

Nancy's friends and Aunt Eloise hurried through the night, determined to make a rescue.

# · 20 ·

## *The Tables Turned*

JOHN HORN trudged on as long as he could, then directed the others how to go. Dave and Burt, the first to reach the cabin, yelled Nancy's name. There was no answer.

Eagerly they charged up to the door. When they failed to open it, Burt said, "Focus your flashlight here, Dave. . . . Padlocked, eh?"

"We'll try a window," his friend suggested. "If necessary, we'll break the glass."

"Hey, is she there? Have you found Nancy?" George called as she and Bess came hurrying up to join the boys. Chuck and Ned were close behind.

"We don't know yet," Dave said. "This door is locked. We're going to try getting in a window."

"All of them are boarded up," Ned recalled. "But we'll get inside if I have to tear this shack apart."

George was using both fists to hammer on the unyielding door. "Nan-cy!" she shouted. "Nancy, it's George. Can you hear me?" There was no response.

Meanwhile, Burt and Dave were working on a window. "Here's a loose board," Burt yelled excitedly. "Pull!"

Snap! It came off so quickly they nearly lost their balance.

Burt played his flashlight inside the cabin. He could not see much in the clutter of furniture.

Dave was already pulling at another board. Together the boys yanked it off and broke the locked window just as Aunt Eloise came up.

"Nancy!" she called fearfully, but the hoped-for response did not come. By this time Ned was through the opening and flashing his light around. Suddenly the beam revealed the girl, lying on the floor, numb with cold and barely conscious.

"Nancy!" he cried.

"I'm—so—glad—you—found me," she whispered faintly. "I'm—so—terribly—sleepy."

One by one the others climbed through the window. Seeing Nancy, tears streamed down Bess's cheeks. "You're—you're all right, aren't you?" she sobbed.

Ned and Dave untied the robes that bound Nancy's hands and ankles.

"Of course she is," George told her cousin.

Aunt Eloise kissed her niece saying, "Don't worry, honey. We'll get you out of here right away. George, where's that Thermos flask?"

Nancy was given a few sips of hot coffee then wrapped in the blanket and carried out through the window. Burt and Dave insisted upon riding Nancy back to the hotel on a "chair" they made by interlocking their fingers.

A sense of relief, together with the stimulant, brought some warmth to Nancy's body. As the group neared the inn, she was able to talk again.

"As soon as we get inside," she said, "call the police. Tell them it was Channing and his friend Dunstan Lake who kidnapped me. Lake is a man!"

"Oh no!" George groaned. "But don't talk now. Save your strength."

"I must say this much," Nancy persisted. "Explain to the police that those men were going to meet Mitzi at a camp somewhere. Dunstan Lake's a short, ugly fellow with beady eyes."

"I'll tell them," Ned promised.

Aunt Eloise would not hear of Nancy's making the long trip to her house. Instead, she engaged a room for her niece and asked Bess to spend the night with her. Nancy was put to bed, and Miss Drew called in the house physician. After he had prescribed treatment, the doctor remarked:

"You had a narrow escape, young lady, but you'll be all right in the morning. Lucky you knew enough to keep exercising, or you might have frozen to death."

Nancy smiled wanly, and very soon was sound asleep. When she awoke the next morning, Bess, fully dressed, was seated beside her, and a breakfast tray stood on the bureau.

"I'm glad you're awake," she said. "How do you feel?"

"Fine. All mended." Nancy hopped out of bed.

After washing her face and combing her hair, she sat down to enjoy some fruit, cereal, and hot chocolate.

"Are you all set for some simply marvellous news?" Bess asked.

"You bet. Don't keep me in suspense."

At that moment there was a knock on the door, and Aunt Eloise walked in with George. They were happy to see that Nancy had fully recovered, and said the anxious boys were waiting downstairs.

"I was just going to tell Nancy the big news," Bess

said. "Listen to this, Nancy. The police have captured the Channings and Dunstan Lake!"

"Honestly? Oh, that's great! I was so afraid—"

"The troopers found their camp," George interrupted. "Nancy, do you realize what this means? That you've rounded up the whole gang, just as you hoped to do."

"With the help of all of you, including the state troopers," Nancy was quick to say. "Did Mitzi and the others confess to everything?"

George shook his head. "They won't own up to one single thing. The way that Channing woman plays innocent makes me furious!"

As Nancy continued to eat, Aunt Eloise remarked, "This place is full of excitement. The Wells Ranch was robbed again last night."

"What! Oh, my goodness!" Nancy cried.

She suddenly took the breakfast tray off her knees and jumped to her feet.

"That experience I had last night must have frozen my brains," she wailed. "Why, I've forgotten the most important evidence of all!"

"What evidence?" George wanted to know.

"The snow statue. Bess, hand me my clothes, quick! And, George, bring the boys up here in five minutes. There's not a moment to lose."

When the youths arrived, Ned demanded to know what all the excitement was about.

Nancy took a deep breath. "I'll tell you. Ned and Chuck, remember when we saw a man ski down Big Hill and wondered why?"

"I sure do. He was crazy."

"Maybe not so crazy as you think," Nancy replied.

"When you and Chuck left me, I saw the man in a white sweater conceal a bulky pouch in one of those big snow statues."

"You did?" Ned cried. "Nancy, why didn't you mention—"

"I was so cold and tired I forgot about it until just now," Nancy confessed. "Let's run down to the lake. Oh, I hope the pouch is still there!"

Before they could leave the room, the telephone rang. Aunt Eloise answered.

"It's police headquarters, Nancy. They want to speak to you," she said, handing over the instrument.

"Miss Drew, this is Chief Wester," came a man's voice. "We have those three suspects in jail, but they're a hard-boiled lot and refuse to admit a thing."

"I can identify them," Nancy said confidently.

"I know you can point out the men as your abductors," said the police chief. "But Mrs Channing demands her release and we haven't any charge against her."

"Just call Mrs Clifton Packer at River Heights," Nancy advised. "The diamond earrings Mitzi Channing is wearing were stolen from her. And the police at Masonville will tell you that Mitzi is wanted there for shoplifting."

"Thanks. You've helped a lot," said the chief. "And, Miss Drew, will you come to headquarters and be present when we question the trio again? I haven't told them that you were rescued."

"I'll drive over this morning," Nancy promised.

She repeated the conversation to her friends and added, "Now, about the snow statue. I suspect that the

Channing fur racket, which hasn't been cleared up, will be revealed in about ten minutes."

"How?" Bess asked, wide eyed.

"When we see what's in that hidden pouch. Why, where are the boys?" she asked, starting out the door.

Aunt Eloise smiled and put a restraining hand on her niece's arm. "They're acting as your deputies, dear. Let's sit here quietly until they return."

It was hard for Nancy to wait, but she knew her aunt was concerned about her. Twenty minutes later they heard pounding footsteps in the corridor and the boys burst into the room.

"*We found it!*" Dave cried.

"Yes sir-ree! Mission accomplished!" Ned said, grinning and waving a bulky, canvas-covered bundle at Nancy.

"Open it!" Bess urged. "I can't wait to see what's inside."

Tensely, the group gathered round while Nancy loosened the cord and peered inside.

"Furs!" George gasped. "Why, it looks like mink."

"It is," Nancy nodded, pulling several soft lustrous pelts from the bag. "We must turn these over to the police at once. I believe they belong to Mr Wells."

Nearing the bottom of the bag, Nancy gave an exclamation of glee. Sewn to one of the pelts was a small tag: *Wells Mink Ranch.*

"Oh, Nancy, you've done it again!" Bess shrieked.

Nancy hardly heard the remark. Her hand had touched a paper at the bottom of the sack. It proved to be one of the stock certificates to which was attached a note:

*Jacques:*
*Made a neat deal on the earrings. Send Bunny Reynolds*
*a dividend to keep her from hollering when she finds out.*
*Sid*

"This is all we need," said Nancy, rising. "Ned, will you come to police headquarters with me?"

"You bet. I drove your car over here this morning."

It took only half an hour to get there. Nancy handed the bag of mink pelts to Chief Wester at once and explained what it held.

"Fine work, Miss Drew," he said as he shook hands with her. The chief suggested that she go into his office for the interview with the prisoners, and that Ned wait for the right moment to bring in the loot.

"I got in touch with Mrs Packer and the Masonville police," the chief went on as he closed the outer office door. "They both confirm what you told us about Mitzi Channing." He called to a guard to bring in the prisoners through the rear-office door.

Upon seeing Nancy, the Channings and Dunstan Lake looked at one another nervously.

"Miss Drew is here to identify you men as her abductors last night," the chief said. "What have you to say for yourselves?"

"Not a thing," Channing managed to say in a tense voice. "I've never seen her before."

"Me neither," Dunstan Lake added, moistening his dry lips.

"What about you, Mrs Channing?" the officer asked.

"I could say a great deal about that meddlesome

little sleuth," Mitzi snapped, glaring at Nancy, "As for your outrageous charges, we deny every one of them."

"Miss Drew has just brought something that may refresh your memories," Chief Wester said coldly.

He flung open the front-office door. "Mr Ned Nickerson, will you come in, please?" he called.

The chief took the pouch from Ned's hands and laid it on his desk. The prisoners stared in stunned silence.

"The evidence in here is enough to convict you," Wester said. "Nancy Drew saw you put this bag in the snow statue not long after the pelts were stolen, Channing, or Jacques Fremont, which I believe is the name you use in Canada."

To Nancy's surprise, it was Mitzi who broke down first. Sobbing, she advised the men to admit their part in the racket.

"It'll go easier with us," she said. "But someday I'll get even with you, Nancy Drew, for what you've done."

The men finally confessed. Lake was the leader and had thought up the scheme of stealing the furs from the various ranches and secreting them in the snow statue while going for another haul.

"Ned and I must be leaving, Chief Wester," said Nancy. "Only I'd like to ask Mr Channing a question first." Turning to the dejected prisoner, she inquired, "Did you send me a telegram and sign my father's name to it?"

"Yes. You were always on our trail and we wanted to get rid of you until we could make our haul and escape. We hoped to catch you alone on your way to the hotel before you phoned your father."

"And one of you was eavesdropping at my aunt's lodge to find out if I was going to the inn?"

"I was," Dunstan Lake admitted as the prisoners were taken away.

The chief thanked Nancy again, then she and Ned started for Aunt Eloise's lodge.

"I guess this ends the *Mystery at the Ski Jump*," Ned remarked as he turned into the camp lane. "It was exciting, but I'll be glad to just sit and talk to you a while. In two days the old grind at Emerson begins again. Nancy, don't you dare get involved in another mystery before the winter carnival at Emerson."

"I promise," the young detective replied laughingly but secretly hoped another mystery would turn up very soon.

It did indeed, and came to be known as *The Spider Sapphire Mystery*.

Nancy and Ned had barely stepped inside the lodge when George cried, "Look! Someone's coming in a car. Could it be John Horn?"

"Not in a car." Bess giggled.

Their visitor was not the old trapper but Mr Drew. He and Nancy embraced joyfully.

"When Aunt Eloise telephoned me you were lost, Nancy," the lawyer said, "I took the first plane I could get. Poor Hannah was frantic too."

"Have you told her I'm all right?" Nancy asked.

"Yes. I phoned her from the inn. She was certainly relieved. And Hannah sent you a message, Nancy. Mitzi's skating partner Smith and that man Ben in New York who printed the Forest Fur Company stock have been arrested."

"Serves them right!" George stated firmly.

"And by the way," Mr Drew went on, "while I was at Longview, I talked to Chuck. John Horn came in too. You'll all be pleased to know that, with the old trapper's sworn testimony, Chuck is sure to regain most of his inheritance. His uncle had put the money into his own bank account, but hadn't spent much of it."

Then Mr Drew smiled at his daughter. "Chuck asked me to deliver a message. He thinks the successful outcome of his case and Nancy's calls for a celebration. He has invited all of you to be his guests at dinner at Longview tomorrow night."

"Hurrah!" Bess shouted. "A party!"

The next morning Mr Drew was obliged to return to River Heights. The young people spent the day enjoying winter sports, then changed to suits and dresses.

When they arrived at the inn they found that Chuck had engaged a small, private dining-room where places were set for ten persons. John Horn and Mr Wells were to join the party. There were colourful favours at each plate and a special menu, with the promise of dancing afterwards. When dessert was brought in, their host rose from his chair.

"This is a happy occasion for me," Chuck announced. "I've not only had gratifying news from my lawyer, Mr Drew, but I've made some grand new friends, among them one of the country's cleverest detectives."

Nancy found herself blushing as the others applauded.

"I've been given the pleasure of making some presentations. Mrs Packer has asked the police to present her diamond brooch to Nancy because of the wonderful way in which she tracked down the thief. And here it is!"

"Oh, Nancy, it's beautiful!" gasped Bess.

"B-but I don't deserve this," the embarrassed girl protested.

"Indeed you do." Chuck smiled. "You deserve it—and more."

As he spoke, the ski instructor laid a gaily wrapped box on the table before Nancy. "This," he told her, "is from Mr Wells, John Horn, and me."

There was a great hush as Nancy lifted the box lid. Inside were several glossy mink pelts—enough to make a lovely stole.

Nancy's eyes were moist with emotion. She did manage to thank them all, saying she would wear the lovely fur piece in remembrance of her adventure at Big Hill.

As the young people rose to attend the dance, Mr Wells called Ned, Burt, and Dave aside. There was a howl of laughter. Then Ned came walking forward with a deer head held in front of his face.

"For our fraternity house, girls. The old deer invites you to come to Emerson and help hang him over the fireplace!"

# Have you seen
# **NANCY DREW**
# lately?

Nancy Drew has become a girl of the 80s! There is hardly a girl from seven to seventeen who doesn't know her name.

Now you can continue to enjoy Nancy Drew in a new series, written for older readers – THE NANCY DREW FILES. Each book has more romance, fashion, mystery and adventure.

In THE NANCY DREW FILES, Nancy pursues one thrilling adventure after another. With her boundless energy and intelligence, Nancy finds herself enrolling at a crime-ridden high school, attending rock concerts and locating the missing star, skiing in Vermont with friends Bess and George and faithful boyfriend Ned, and temping at a teenage magazine based in wildly exciting New York.

## COMING IN SPRING 1988

## **The Nancy Drew Files**

**No. 1 Secrets Can Kill**
**No. 2 Deadly Intent**
**No. 3 Murder on Ice**
**No. 4 Smile and Say Murder**

ARMADA

# Armadas

Here are some of the most recent titles
in our exciting fiction series:

The Chalet School and Rosalie  *Elinor M. Brent-Dyer* £1.75
The Secret of the Forgotten City  *Carolyn Keene* £1.95
The Masked Monkey  *Franklin W. Dixon* £1.95
The Mystery of the Creep-Show Crooks  *M. V. Carey* £1.95
Horse of Fire  *Patricia Leitch* £1.75
Cry of a Seagull  *Monica Dickens* £1.75
The Secret of Moon Castle  *Enid Blyton* £1.95
Legion of the Dead  *J. H. Brennan* £1.95

Armada paperbacks are available in
bookshops and newsagents, but can
also be ordered by post.

# How to Order

Please send the purchase price plus 22p per book (maximum postal charge £3.00) to Armada Paperbacks, Cash Sales Dept., GPO Box 29, Douglas, Isle of Man. Please use cheque, postal or money order – do not send currency.

NAME (Block letters) .................................................

ADDRESS ................................................................

.............................................................................

.............................................................................